A COUNTRY MOUSE

Emily Gibson is a spirited young woman who wishes to make her own way in life. She has been looking after her family since her father died, but with mounting debts something must be done. Deciding that she must marry for money, she writes to ask her estranged grandfather, the Earl of Westerham, to put forward an appropriate suitor. But he selects her cousin — and he's the last person Emily would have chosen. Can love blossom in such circumstances?

Books by Fenella Miller
in the Linford Romance Library:

THE RETURN OF LORD RIVENHALL

FENELLA MILLER

A COUNTRY MOUSE

Complete and Unabridged

LINFORD
Leicester

First published in Great Britain in 2007

First Linford Edition
published 2008

British Library CIP Data

Miller, Fenella-Jane
  A country mouse.—Large print ed.—
  Linford romance library
  1. Arranged marriage—Fiction
  2. Love stories 3. Large type books
  I. Title
  823.9'2 [F]

  ISBN 978–1–84782–185–0

Published by
F. A. Thorpe (Publishing)
Anstey, Leicestershire

Set by Words & Graphics Ltd.
Anstey, Leicestershire
Printed and bound in Great Britain by
T. J. International Ltd., Padstow, Cornwall

This book is printed on acid-free paper

1

'Mama, shall I arrange to have the roof mended or not?' Emily waited, fists clenched, for her mother, the Lady Althea Gibson, to reply.

'What was that, my love?'

'The roof, Mama, shall I get it repaired?' Her mother frowned and closed her eyes again.

'Whatever you please, my love. You know best.'

Emily watched her mother sink back into a deep sleep and her eyes filled. It had been so different two years ago, before her father had been killed in a carriage accident. Then, Glebe House, had been a happy place; her mother lively and beautiful.

Now she lay on the *chaise-longue* all day, taking no interest in anything, making no decisions, leaving everything to Emily. Her mother was only two and forty but looked years older. Her lovely brown hair was fading and her skin held an unhealthy pallor. She realized she was watching her mother slowly fade away but there was nothing she could do about it.

Her father, Mr Peter Gibson, had died, taking his annuity with him. The small estate produced barely enough revenue to keep herself, her mother, and her two younger sisters, Amelia aged thirteen and Serena aged nine, from penury. Emily sighed and crossed the room to pull up the patchwork comforter, her mother's skeletal frame barely making a dent in the cover, then she returned to the study to continue her efforts at finding a way to keep their small family afloat.

'Em, are you coming for a walk with us? Mary says we can go and look for blackberries in the woods.' Serena already had her cloak and walking boots on ready for the promised outing.

'No, Serena, I'm sorry, I have too much to attend to this morning. But I will be up this afternoon to see how well you have learnt yesterday's lessons.' Emily reached down and refastened Serena's bonnet string. The early autumn weather was fine, but since her younger sister's near fatal illness two winters before, she had remained susceptible to chills and fevers.

Serena grinned up at Emily. 'Millie has not finished her French so you had better not come up before teatime.' There was a clatter of boots on the uncarpeted stairs behind them.

'I *have* finished; do not tell tales, Serena. I did it just now.'

'I am delighted to hear it, Millie.' Emily kissed her sister and automatically rectified her appearance. 'Must you always look so harum-scarum, my dear? If you travelled about the place a little more slowly I'm certain you would get less dishevelled.'

Amelia Gibson was at that stage when she appeared to be all legs and arms and flying hair. But even at thirteen her oval face, with its huge violet eyes, framed by tumbling nut-brown curls, gave promise that she would be a great beauty in years to come.

Millie shook her head, dislodging several more strands of hair from what was meant to be a tidy waist-length braid. 'I like to run, Em; I would never have time enough to do all the things I wish to do in a day if I walked everywhere, as you do.'

'I'm a responsible adult of almost twenty years. I can hardly race about Glebe House. Mama would be scandalized.' They all knew their beloved mother scarcely noticed their existence but Emily liked to pretend things were as they should be. She would do anything to make life easier for Serena and Millie and her mother.

Mary, the girls' nurse, appeared, a trifle breathless, from the narrow servants passageway. 'Goodness me, Miss Millie, you fair wear me out! I can scarce keep up with you.'

'Then don't try, Mary. We're quite

content to wait for you.' Mary had nursed all three of the Gibson girls with love and devotion but was now, in her middle years, finding the energetic Millie a sore trial to her plump legs.

'It's unladylike to run downstairs, Miss Millie, and well you know it.'

Fearing another argument Serena intervened. She slipped her hand into Mary's. 'Mary, shall we go and fetch a basket from Cook? If we're to pick blackberries we will need something to put them in, will we not?'

'I'll run and get one. Wait here for me.' Millie was gone, with a flurry of fading blue calico and crisp starched cotton, leaving them no choice.

Emily laughed. 'It's no good fretting, Mary. Millie will grow out of it; after all I did, did I not?' She watched the three depart, chattering happily, down the weed filled drive, and closed the heavy oak front door, returning to her duties. It seemed a lifetime since she had either the freedom, or the inclination, to dash about the place.

The past two years had been grey and oppressive. Angrily she slammed the study door behind her. Her maternal grandfather, the Earl of Westerham, was entirely to blame for their present miserable situation.

Her mother, Althea, had been born unexpectedly to the Countess when in her forties, and had been much petted and spoilt by both doting parents. Her older brother, Peregrine, had already left home and married when his parents presented him with an infant sister. He viewed the whole proceedings with extreme distaste and had never exchanged more than a few words with his sibling.

When Althea married, against the wishes of her parents, one Mr Peter Gibson, a country squire of impeccable birth but moderate income, her parents had been displeased. However all might have been well if the Countess had not died soon afterwards before they could be reconciled. The Earl blamed his daughter for his wife's death and never forgave her.

Whilst her father had been alive, Emily knew her mother had been able to contain her grief at the Earl's harsh treatment, but now the misery of losing her husband had uncovered the old wound and it was proving too much for her. Lady Althea was suffering from a nervous condition, which became worse as each day passed, which had started after she had become a widow.

Emily had written to her grandfather, telling him of her father's death, and her mother's poor health, but had received no response. She knew there was no point applying to her Uncle Peregrine for he had died many years ago. She supposed that she must have cousins and second cousins but the connection was too distant to be of any use to her now.

Her spirits sank when she looked at the pile of papers on the desk. All demands for payment and she had scarcely enough funds to cover them. And now the roof had sprung a leak and there was nothing she could do about it. At this rate Glebe House would fall down around their ears before they had the wherewithal to repair it.

She sank back on one of the threadbare, sagging chairs and her shoulders slumped. What could she do? Was there no way out or did certain ruin face them? Where could she obtain the necessary money to solve their problems?

Suddenly she sat up; clapping her hands to her mouth as an incredible idea occurred to her. Yes; it was the only way. She would find a wealthy man and marry him. She frowned as a potential problem occurred to her. She didn't know any men wealthy or otherwise. But she knew someone who did!

She scrambled up and hurried over to the desk. She pushed the pile of bills to one side and placed a clean sheet of paper in front of her. She would write, one last time, to her grandfather. He was, after all, her guardian, and the head of her household, even if so far he had ignored his duties.

She carefully trimmed a quill and prepared to write the most difficult letter of her life. She was going to ask her grandfather, the Earl of Westerham, to find her a suitable husband. Years ago he had arranged a match for his daughter, Althea, but she had refused his choice. Perhaps his granddaughter's willingness to be married to a man that he selected would heal the breach between the families.

If her mother had been well Emily would not have contemplated such a drastic step but in the present circumstances she doubted that her decision would be questioned.

★ ★ ★

'Have you taken leave of your senses, my lord?' The Right Honourable, Sebastian Edward Lessing, the Viscount Yardley, looked down his long aristocratic nose at his great-grandfather, the Earl of Westerham, seated comfortably in front of a roaring apple wood fire.

'Sit down, my boy, and stop glaring at me. I have merely suggested that you consider marrying my granddaughter, Emily Gibson. I do not see why you are so outraged.'

The tall, elegant young man, kicked viciously at a log in the grate, making the sparks shoot up the wide chimney. 'I have no desire to become leg shackled, my lord. I have my duties in the government to perform. Taking a wife in such circumstances would be the height of folly. Good God, sir, I am hardly in the country at the moment. Since Boney escaped from Elba I could be sent abroad at any moment, surely you understand that?'

'Exactly, my boy, and what happens if you are killed? I know you are a diplomat, but you are often at the front line of battle, are you not?' Reluctantly Sebastian nodded. 'You have no heir, with your death the title would die out, would you have that happen?'

'No, of course not.' Sebastian turned,

flicked a piece of ash from his glossy top boots, and strolled back to stare unhappily out of the window. Acres of lush parkland rolled away from him. Westerham had been in the Lessing family for hundreds of years; he owed it to his ancestors to ensure it remained so. He supposed great-grandfather was correct; he really had no choice. He needed to marry and set up his nursery.

'Very well, sir; I accept that I need to find a wife. But why my second cousin Emily? I did not know of her existence until five minutes ago. And what makes you suppose she would wish to marry me?'

The Earl chuckled and his harsh features softened. 'Here, my boy, read this.' He waved a much crumpled piece of paper in front of Sebastian who reached over and took it. He read the missive with growing astonishment. His finally arched eyebrows disappeared under his fashionably cropped hair. His voice dripped with disdain.

'Emily Gibson, my lord, is outrageous.

To offer herself up for sale in this manner shows a lack of refinement and breeding I could not countenance in a wife of mine.'

'How dare you insult my grand-daughter, Yardley. I will not have a word said against Emily.' The Earl glared at his great-grandson until the younger man flushed and looked away. Sebastian did not offer an apology. 'It is my fault, you see; I blamed her mother for my wife's death. The child wrote to me two years ago begging for my assistance when her father died but I ignored her appeal.' The old man openly wiped his eyes. 'I am head of the family; it is my job to take care of them. I have been very remiss not to have done so before. I want to be reconciled with my daughter, Althea, before I meet my maker.'

Sebastian snorted. 'Well and good, sir. You can do that without involving me in your plans, can you not?'

'I am four and eighty, my boy, and however robust I appear, I can not have long left on this earth. You wish to find a wife, my granddaughter wishes to find a husband, what better arrangement could there be?'

'I could select a wife for myself.'

'When do you have the opportunity? You are not part of the fashionable set, you do not attend Almack's, or debutante balls, how are you going to meet someone more suitable, tell me that?'

Sebastian shook his head in frustration. He could feel himself being pushed into a corner. Then unexpectedly he smiled. 'Very well, my lord. I will agree to meet this young woman, but if she is not to my liking, I reserve the right to refuse. Is that acceptable?'

The Earl of Westerham smiled back. 'Excellent! I am sure Emily will be a lovely girl; her mother was a diamond of the first water at her age. She is certainly resourceful and intelligent. Her letters to me are proof of that at least.'

'When do you wish me to return to

inspect the girl?'

'I intend to send my carriage for them today; it is to be hoped they would be here by the end of the week. There are two younger girls as well. It will be wonderful to hear the sound of children about this huge empty place once more.'

Sebastian shuddered. He had three unknown country cousins to contend with? What a lowering thought; if he decided to marry the eldest, Emily, he supposed he would be expected to provide for the other two as well. He had no dealings with children and desired to keep it that way for as long as possible.

'I must return to town, sir. I am wanted in Cabinet. I will endeavour to visit Westerham sometime next week.'

The two men, so alike in both appearance and personality that they constantly clashed, parted, for once, on amicable terms. Two hours after Viscount Yardley's departure an enormous crested travelling carriage, complete with coachman, groom and two postilions, lumbered out, followed by an empty baggage cart and two armed outriders. No one with any sense risked the roads without adequate protection from highwaymen and footpads.

* * *

From her hidden position at the study window Emily watched the impressive carriage trundle up their rutted drive, her heart pounding with apprehension. Her grandfather had responded to her letter in a way she had not anticipated.

She heard pounding, childish footsteps approaching down the corridor. The study door burst open and Millie and Serena erupted into the room. 'Em come and see. There's a huge crested coach coming down the drive. Whoever can it be? Do we know anyone like that?'

Emily swallowed. 'Yes, my love, we do. Don't you remember that our grandfather is the Earl of Westerham?

That is why mother is known as Lady Althea Gibson, not Mrs Gibson.'

'But Mama does not speak to him. How can he be here?' Millie's voice was shrill.

'Calm yourself, Amelia, and I'll explain.' Emily waited for her sisters to be quiet. 'I wrote to grandfather explaining that Mama was unwell and asked him if he could help in any way.' Never would she admit to her sisters, or her mother, the true contents of her letter.

'And he has come himself? Do you think he's in the coach?' Serena piped.

'No, darling, I'm sure he is not. He must be well over eighty now. I'm certain he would never travel so far.'

'Then who is it? Why's the coach coming here?'

'Amelia, don't be so impatient. I have no more idea than you do. Now run along and tell Edwards; she will wish to prepare Mama.' She took Serena's hand. 'You stay with me; we will go and wait in the morning room together.'

Scarcely ten minutes later a loud knocking was heard on the front door. The one remaining maid-servant, Sally, hurried to answer the summons. Outside stood an impressive array of people. A black garbed gentleman headed the queue.

'Is Lady Althea Gibson, at home?'

The girl dropped a nervous curtsy. 'Yes, sir, that she is. Will you come in, please? Who will I tell her is waiting?'

'Mr Foster, the Earl of Westerham's man of business. I have a letter for Miss Emily Gibson and one for Lady Althea. Deliver them for me please.'

'Please to wait in the ante-room, sir. I will take the letters directly.' The frightened girl left Mr Foster in the small room next to the entrance hall. She hesitated, not sure if the waiting grooms and outriders should be directed elsewhere.

'My staff will wait outside.'

'Yes, Mr Foster, sir, thank you.' The girl hastily closed the door and scuttled across the shabby hall to find Miss

Emily. She knew Lady Althea was asleep in her bed, even though it was past noon.

'I have two letters here, Miss Emily.'

'Thank you, I shall take them both. Could you take in some refreshment for our visitor?'

With shaking hands she broke the impressive seal and unfolded the letter. Her youngest sister watched anxiously as the colour drained from Emily's face.

'What is it, Em, is it bad news? Has our grandfather died?'

Emily pulled herself together sufficiently to answer. 'No, darling. It's very good news indeed. Grandfather has invited us all to live with him at Westerham. He is to take care of us in future. Is that not splendid news?'

2

Serena wondered why such good news had caused her elder sister to look so frightened. 'Don't you wish to go, Em?'

'Yes, of course, I do. It's a shock; but a welcome one.' She bent down to hug her sister. 'It has been such a worry, trying to keep us solvent on so little money. When I wrote to the Earl I had no idea he would respond so quickly. That's why I was unnerved for a moment, nothing more, I do assure you, sweetheart.'

'Shall I run and tell Mama? She was always used to talk about Westerham and what a great house it was, when Papa was alive. She will be pleased to return, won't she?'

'I'm sure she will. But don't go upstairs to tell her; I will come along directly I have spoken to Mr Foster. She was still asleep a little while ago. It will take time for Edwards to get her organized. We don't wish to make her even more unwell do we, Serena?'

The little girl solemnly shook her head, her dark braids flying. 'Can I tell Millie though?'

Emily gave her consent and the child ran off, eager to share the amazing news with someone. Mr Foster stood up as Emily entered. He bowed.

'I am delighted to meet you, Miss Gibson.' He didn't offer his hand and Emily did not curtsy, she merely nodded politely. She might be as poor as a country mouse but she knew how to behave.

'I have read my letter, Mr Foster. It will take us a few days to get ready for a move to Westerham.'

'Of course it will, Miss Gibson. I have arranged to put up at the Bull, in the next village. I will leave a groom here, if that's acceptable. Please send word with him when you're ready to depart.'

Emily agreed she would do that. An

extra pair of strong male hands would be a boon moving trunks and belongings down to the hall. Glebe House no longer had male indoor servants. She had had to let them go when her father passed away.

She picked up her skirts and ran lightly upstairs, the letter for her mother in her other hand. The one addressed to herself was burning a hole in her pocket. She felt her colour rise as she remembered its contents. The Earl had offered the Gibson family his protection and wished for them to come and live with him at Westerham. He had also agreed to find her a suitable husband but suggested that it would meet with his wholehearted approval if she agreed to marry his great-grandson, his heir, her second cousin, Sebastian Edward Lessing, Viscount Yardley.

She knew little of the man, apart from he was four and twenty years old and already a respected diplomat. She also knew that he lived in London, so must suppose he was a member of the *ton*, a Corinthian, and a man of taste and wealth. After all he had been living on his expectations for years as both his father, and grandfather, had predeceased the Earl of Westerham.

She smiled ruefully at her faded grey gown, twice made over, and sadly in need of renewal. Whatever would a fashionable man about town see in such a country mouse as she?

She stopped dead, clutching the banister for support as an appalling thought occurred to her. What if her cousin found her not to his taste and refused to marry her? Would they all be sent packing? Be returned to live in Glebe House? Fervently she prayed, as she stood frozen halfway up the stairs. 'Oh God, please do not let him refuse me. It would kill Mama if she was to be restored to her family home and then rejected for a second time.' She felt a chill run down her spine at another unwelcome thought.

Her mother had been so ill these last

two years, spending most of her days lying unseeing and uncaring on her day bed. Her nights she spent in a laudanum induced sleep. How would the man, hard enough to have rejected his only daughter for marrying against his wishes, react to her changed condition?

They couldn't go to Westerham until her mother was more herself. She determined to persuade her mother to try and return to the real world; Emily continued her journey upstairs, the light of battle in her amazing hazel eyes.

★   ★   ★

Edwards, Lady Althea's dresser, had succeeded in rousing her. 'Come along now, my lady, up you get. There's a letter here for you. It's a long time since we had a letter isn't it?' Edwards' mention of the letter had been the key.

'What is that, Edwards? A letter did you say? Hand it to me, please.' Lady Althea Gibson pushed her stringy hair back from her pale forehead, quite unconcerned about her appearance. In her youth she had been in the forefront of fashion but nowadays she scarcely noticed what she wore or how she looked. She just did not have the energy to cope with life without her beloved Peter. But a letter? Now that *was* worth waking up for. That her daughters were lost without her had long ago ceased to be a concern.

She was ineffectually struggling to pick off the impressive blob of sealing wax when something about its shape and imprint caused her to pause. 'It is from Papa! Edwards, this is from my Papa.'

With shaky fingers she unfolded the stiff paper and began to read. For a moment the heavy black scrawl she knew so well danced before her eyes. With a supreme effort she focused and began to read.

My dear daughter, Althea,
    It has been far too long since we

are on good terms. I admit the fault has been mine and wish to make amends, if you will allow me to. I have sent a carriage to collect you and your three girls. I would like you all to move to Westerham and live with me.

Your father,
Richard Lessing.

Althea felt her stomach roil and was glad she had not eaten. She raised her head and her eyes were full. 'Edwards, I am to go home. He has asked me to come home. At last, I shall have back the life that I lost.'

'I'm delighted, madam. That's good news indeed. But if we're to travel sixty miles you'll need to feel well. At the moment you're not strong enough to stand the journey.'

Before Lady Althea could answer Emily entered, her pale serious face for once animated and her remarkable eyes sparkling. 'Mama, have you read your letter yet?'

'I have, my dear. Your grandfather has invited us to make his home with him. Are you not pleased?

'I am, of course I am. But there is much to do before we can depart. The carriage and staff that accompanied it are going to put up at The Bull, in Misham. We're to send for them when we're ready. I have told them that we'll need several days. Is that going to be sufficient for you, Mama?' This was addressed at her mother but it was at Edwards that she looked. Her mother's devoted dresser nodded and Emily's smile became broader.

'I should think it would do, my dear. But I must have some new gowns before we leave. It will not do for Papa to think me dowdy.'

'I have already sent to Misham and Mrs Simpson will be here later. Jenny's upstairs in the attics at this very moment collecting the last of the Indian materials we have been saving for such an occasion as this,' Emily told her.

Her mother frowned. 'I will require at

least three gowns; you and the girls must make do with one. I doubt that there will be enough material left for you to have more.

'It's of no matter, Mama. I'll be content to have one new gown, I can assure you.' Emily hoped that it was true that first impressions were what mattered. She would wear her new gown to make her first curtsy, after that she would have to return to her meagre wardrobe, and she knew nobody would be impressed by that.

Lady Althea watched the play of emotion across her eldest daughter's face. 'I shall ask Mrs Simpson to make you and the girls two dresses each; it is essential that we all have at least one change of raiment.' Exhausted she sank back on her pillows. She opened her eyes again with difficulty, and reached over to take her daughter's hand. 'I shall try harder, my love. I shall not be like this any longer. I will be your old mother again presently. Wait and see.'

Emily returned the squeeze and bent

to kiss her mother's cheek. 'I know you will, Mama, and I will help you. But it's going to take time to restore you to your former health. You must not expect to be back to normal in a week or so; you have been ill for two years, and it could be months before you're feeling quite well. But for the moment you must think about eating again and getting up and moving around your room. You have been lying still for far too long.'

But her mother was once more asleep, and had not heard her. Emily turned to Edwards, her eyes hard. 'Give me the laudanum, Edwards. There will be no more.'

'But, Miss Emily, her ladyship cannot sleep without it. She'll be in desperate straits if you take it away.' Emily continued to hold out her hand and reluctantly the elderly woman went to retrieve the three small bottles of black, noxious fluid from their hiding place. 'Whatever you may think, miss, your dear mother would not be alive today without that.'

'I know you're probably correct and I'm sorry Edwards. It's not your fault. But I hate to see her this way.'

'Leave me a little then, miss, for when she becomes too restless; it's best to stop it gradually, you know.'

Emily hesitated, unwilling to give the evil liquid back. But Edwards was right; her mother would have died from grief without the pain being dulled by opium. She examined the three small bottles. 'You may have this, it's half full. But it's to be the last, be very sure of that.'

'Once Lady Althea is back home she will not need it anymore. Wait and see, Miss Gibson, madam will regain her former spirits in no time.'

'I pray that you're correct. Try and get her up and dressed; the girls will wish to see her later on. They're bursting with questions about Westerham.'

★   ★   ★

The intervening days were filled with feverish activity. Trunks were found and packed with favourite books and leisure items. Mrs Simpson and her team of seamstresses snipped and sewed with enthusiasm and produced the required garments in record time. Their arrival was greeted with speechless admiration. Lady Althea, although still too weak to remain on her feet all day, was making a valiant effort. It was she who broke the silence.

'Mrs Simpson, you have surpassed yourself. The gowns are beautiful. I had no notion that the Indian silk would make up so well in that new high waisted style.'

The mantua maker bobbed a curtsy, beaming happily at her customer's delight. 'Yes, my lady, such delicate material is perfect for the long flowing skirts. There was sufficient left over to make matching shawls and even trim your bonnets.' Her assistants held up the items for their inspection.

'Mama, you'll look wonderful in that

gown. Burgundy and gold are a perfect combination,' Emily exclaimed, pleased her mother was taking an interest in her appearance once more. 'And I like the long sleeves and high neckline. Your old burgundy pelisse is an exact match and now that it has been taken in, it will complete your outfit perfectly.'

Serena and Amelia examined the dresses made for them from a length of blue and white muslin. They even had new pinafores and stockings. 'Thank you, Em, I love my dresses.' Millie ran the material of one through her fingers enjoying its softness. 'And your lilac and silver gown is beautiful too.'

'I know, Millie. I was not sure such a colour combination was entirely suitable for someone my age, but it does look lovely. I think this new fashion is very flattering, especially for someone who is as tall and thin as I am.'

'The colour is very becoming, my dear,' Lady Althea said, noticing for the first time how much weight her eldest daughter had shed.

The outfits to be worn on the journey were hung ready for the following day and the others carefully packed, in tissue paper, in the waiting trunks. Glebe House was to be closed down; Holland sheets covered all the furniture and the shutters were locked. Cook and her husband Potts, the sole outdoor man, were to remain behind to act as caretakers.

As all their horses had been sold there were no grooms or stable boys to find employment for. Mary, the girls' nurse, and Jenny, Emily's abigail and Edwards, her mother's dresser, were obviously to accompany them. Sally, the one remaining live in servant, had found employment locally. The daily women, who came to do the heavy cleaning and laundry, had been given a guinea as compensation.

Everything was as it should be. Emily was still concerned that her mother was too frail to cope with the rigours of a two-day journey but Lady Althea assured her she was stout enough to travel.

Five days after the luxurious coach had first appeared at Glebe House it returned to collect the Gibson family. Their baggage had departed the previous day; it would be waiting for them when they arrived at Westerham. Now the moment for departure had come the family was silent. The girls stopped their excited chattering; Emily felt her chest constrict, but Lady Althea was only worried that her beloved father would not welcome her as she hoped. The house she had spent half her life in was no longer somewhere she wished to be. It held too many sad memories, and was a daily reminder of her insurmountable loss.

Foster would ride on the box with the coachman. It would be unseemly for him to travel inside even if there was sufficient room. He had been obliged to hire a second carriage to transport the three servants. He had expected them to travel with the baggage but Miss Gibson had refused to agree to this. She had insisted that they could not manage a two-day journey without their personal maids.

The steps were folded back and the carriage door slammed shut. Foster sprung up on to the box and the coachman gave the four handsome matching bays the office to start.

'Well, we're off. I can hardly believe we're leaving Glebe House for ever.' Millie said, quietly. Emily shivered. She could not bear to consider the possibility that she would be found wanting by Viscount Yardley and they would all be sent back.

Lady Althea fell into a fitful doze and Amelia and Serena were happy watching the blaze of autumn colour pass by their window. Emily was allowed to sit undisturbed and contemplate the future. What did Sebastian look like? Was he handsome? Would he be a considerate husband? She smiled as she remembered how happy her parents had been. She wanted her union to be a loving relationship like that. She swallowed as bile rose in her throat.

Her marriage would never be the same; it was to be one of convenience; Viscount Yardley needed to set up his nursery before he left for the continent and she was marrying to provide security for her family.

Exactly what was involved in 'setting up a nursery', she had only the vaguest notion of. Whatever it was, she knew, she was not looking forward to it. These unpleasant thoughts were interrupted by her mother, who had woken.

'Are you quite well, Emily, my dear? You have gone very white? I hope you are not feeling travel sick?'

'No, I'm fine. Just a little apprehensive about starting a new life. You're going home, Mama; Westerham is entirely new to us.'

'You are all going to love it; I was so happy there. In some parts it dates back hundreds of years, you know. My grandfather had a new wing built in the modern style and it is in this part that we shall reside.' She closed her eyes and her mouth curved as she thought about her childhood home. 'It has bathing rooms attached to the main suites where one can take a bath whenever one wishes. Only the hot water has to be fetched up; the dirty water escapes down a pipe.'

The two younger girls looked at their mother in astonishment. 'But where does the water go to, Mama?' Serena asked.

'I have no idea, darling. I only know it disappears.'

'I expect it is directed outside,' Emily told the girls. 'We shall have to investigate when we arrive.'

Foster had arranged for them to break their journey for nuncheon at The Bell, a prestigious posting house. The food provided was the best they had eaten for more than two years. Replete and happy they all snoozed the afternoon away. The overnight stop was equally enjoyable, for only Lady Althea would ever have experienced such fawning and bowing as they were offered.

The best of everything had been bespoken and they were given the attention such expense merited. Serena and Millie were almost sorry when the carriage turned into the impressive stone gates and began the final stage of their trip down the three miles of impeccably tended drive.

The length of this, and the splendour of the park, silenced even the girls. Lady Althea's head turned eagerly, noting changes and recognizing landmarks she had not seen for twenty-two years. Emily sat, staring straight ahead, feeling more nauseous by the minute. She wished that she could vanish from the silk-lined coach and miraculously return to Glebe House.

She realized that her decision to sacrifice her own happiness to provide security for her sisters was not going to be easy. The nearer they got to their destination the more frightened she became. She wished she had not eaten so heavily at breakfast.

'Stop; please — stop.' She banged frantically on the coach roof and the vehicle lurched to a standstill. Not waiting for the steps, Emily threw open the door, jumped down, and ran for the privacy of the bushes where she cast up her accounts; she was watched with concern by her mother, amusement by her sisters but disgust by the man, mounted on a magnificent chestnut stallion, his presence hidden by the overhanging branches of the yew trees.

3

Jenny, seeing her mistress's distress, scrambled down from her place in the following carriage. Emily finished her retching and wiped her mouth on the damp cloth Jenny handed to her. Her head was spinning and her knees weak. 'Thank you, Jenny. I am recovered now.'

She stepped away from the bushes and stood whilst her maid attempted to restore order to her appearance. She glanced up to see three anxious faces watching from the carriage. Pinning a smile to her pale face she walked back and climbed slowly up the steps that had been lowered in her absence by one of the postilions.

'I'm so sorry, Mama. I do believe that something I ate at breakfast must have disagreed with me.'

'And I am sorry, my dear. I should have got down to assist you. But I am no use in such circumstances, as you well know.'

'Please do not apologise, Mama. I'm quite old enough to vomit on my own.' She heard a smothered giggle. 'It's quite permissible to laugh girls. I'm not so stuffy as to object.'

Amelia grinned. 'You were very sick, Em; I'm so relieved that you got out of the carriage in time.'

Emily joined in the laughter. 'Amen to that, Millie.' She reached up, tapped gently, on the roof, and the carriage resumed its stately process down the drive.

★   ★   ★

Whilst the girls exclaimed in wonder at the extent of the rolling parkland and the handsome trees both Emily and Lady Althea sat silently, immersed in their own thoughts. Lady Althea had no reservations about her return to Westerham. It was where she belonged now that her husband was no longer alive.

40

She had accepted her reduced circumstances happily when she was sharing them with her beloved Peter. Without him the misery of her penury had quite overwhelmed her.

She knew that now she had returned she would get well again and be able to take her place in society. Lady Althea glanced down at her new dress and her thin lips curved in appreciation. Soon her father would replenish the whole of her wardrobe and she could start re-establishing herself in the *ton*. The season had barely begun; in a few weeks she was certain that she would be strong enough to enjoy escorting Emily to the balls, soirées, and musical evenings on offer in London.

Emily's thoughts were not so sanguine. Her mother's happiness, maybe her very life, was dependent on her fulfilling her grandfather's wishes. She had no doubt that his benevolence was linked to her marriage to his heir, the Viscount Yardley. If he had truly wished to restore their fortunes he could have done so two years since, when he received the first letter asking for help.

She looked across at her mother, so thin and frail, but at least she was smiling. Edwards had assured her Lady Althea was no longer taking laudanum every night to help her sleep. Everything rested on Emily's shoulders. Well, they were strong enough; she had been running Glebe House, and educating her sisters, for the past two years. She doubted that many 19-year-olds could do as she had done. Compared to that, persuading her cousin Sebastian to make an offer should present no difficulty.

'Em, Emily, look, look at the house! It looks just like a castle.' Serena tugged at her sister's sleeve to gain her attention.

'Sorry, Serena, I was wool-gathering. Are we there?' Emily leaned forward and peered out of the window. 'Good heavens, it's huge! And you never said it was half castle, Mama.'

'Did I not, my dear, I must have

forgot.' Her mother joined them at the open window. 'It is exactly as I remember it. I am so glad that I am back here at last. I have missed Westerham every day I have been away.'

Emily's brow creased a little. Was her mother's enthusiasm unnatural? Surely all young women understood they had to leave the familial home when they embarked on matrimony? Was this obsession with Westerham a sign that she was still unwell after her prolonged period of mental instability?

'Well, you're home now, Mama. I cannot wait for you to show us all the places that you have talked about so much.'

Her mother finally focused on her eldest daughter. 'You still look a trifle hagged, my dear. Pinch your cheeks and press your lips together; try and restore some colour to your face. You want to make a good impression, do you not?' Lady Althea smiled and for the first time in two years humour was reflected in her eyes. 'I believe that one pallid individual is quite enough for this family, do not you?'

Emily laughed out loud; the relief at her mother's return to normality replacing her anxiety about making a favourable impression. 'We do look like a pair of underfed sparrows, don't we? But I'm certain will both be robust again now that we're here.'

'There're dozens of footmen waiting outside to greet us, Em. They look like soldiers on parade with all that green and gold frogging,' Amelia commented in awe.

'Do I have to speak to them?' Serena sounded anxious, as the horses dropped to a sedate walk.

'No, darling; you merely nod and smile at servants. Never offer your hand, curtsy or say thank you. It is not done, you know.'

'Not say thank you, Mama? That's so impolite. Emily has always told us we have to treat our staff with respect.'

'That was all very well, Serena, at Glebe House. But here, at Westerham, things are done differently. You do not want the staff to consider you ignorant, do you?' Serena shook her head, all her pleasure squashed by her mother's words. She shrunk up against Emily's side and pushed her cold hand into her sister's. Emily squeezed it and tried to smile. It was not a very convincing effort.

The coach shuddered to a halt and there was instant activity. Two footmen jumped forward, one opened the door whilst the other pulled the steps into position. The three girls sat immobile, but Lady Althea surged forward. Regally she held out her hand and a footman took it and guided her to the ground. He bowed again, she nodded. Without waiting to see if her daughters followed she walked forward, nodding from time to time, her head high, the ostrich plumes on her bonnet bobbing as she went.

Emily realized they had to move. 'Come along, girls, we're getting left behind.' She stood up and, still clasping

Serena's hand stepped out, ignoring the bowing footman. She waited, back straight, for Amelia to jump down after her, and set off, not wishing her mother to vanish and leave them alone, surrounded by a sea of unfriendly, supercilious servants.

Millie had taken her other hand and now she was obliged to negotiate a flight of intimidating marble steps, flanked by Doric pillars, with no hand available to hold up her skirts. She attempted to extract one hand from Millie's but her sisters fingers tightened.

Drawing a steadying breath Emily prepared to negotiate the front steps without treading on her hem. Somehow she managed to lift her dress a little with her finger tips, in spite of her sisters, and she prayed that she would not fall flat on her face. All was well until the last two steps when a formidable, grey-haired figure, stepped out and bowed deeply.

His sudden appearance startled the

already nervous girls and they both stepped backwards, attempting to hide themselves behind Emily's slender frame, jerking her arms and dislodging her tenuous grip on her skirt. The flimsy stuff of her dress swayed freely and with her next step she trapped it under her boot. Unable to free her hands to balance, Emily fell forward, taking both girls with her, to land in an ignominious heap at the feet of the autocratic butler, Penfold.

Unaware that her humiliation was being observed from the gallery that overlooked the enormous marble floored Grand Hall, Emily disentangled herself from her sisters and staggered to her feet. Not one of the watching servants had stepped forward to assist them and of her mother was no sign. She had vanished into the interior intent on re-establishing herself as her father's 'darling girl'.

The row of footmen remained as statues, faces expressionless, watching her smooth down her dress. 'Are you hurt, Serena, sweetheart? Did I tread on your hand?'

'No, I'm fine, thank you, Emily,' Serena whispered.

'I'm unhurt as well, thank you,' Amelia's voice was thread-thin in the silence. Emily's embarrassment vanished. What sort of an establishment was this, which treated guests so insolently?

She stiffened and met the haughty stare of Penfold. It was his eyes that dropped first. He flushed and bowed again. This time his action was deferential. 'Miss Gibson, Miss Amelia and Miss Serena, welcome to Westerham. His Lordship is waiting to greet you in the green withdrawing-room, if you will kindly follow me.'

Emily was not having this. She was not going to be summoned like a servant before being allowed to recover from her travels. 'We will be shown to our rooms, now, if you please. I shall attend on his lordship when we are recovered from our journey.' She raised an eyebrow and Penfold knew he had met his match.

'Very well, Miss Gibson.' He snapped a finger and two footmen stepped forward. 'Show Miss Gibson, and Miss Amelia and Miss Serena, to their apartments.'

He bowed again to Emily. 'If you would like to ring when you are ready, Miss Gibson? I shall send someone to escort you down.'

Emily nodded, but did not deign to reply. Holding her torn skirt firmly in one hand, the other resting on the polished banister, Emily followed one footman. Her sisters, following her lead, straightened their backs, held their heads high and marched up the stairs, side by side, showing their solidarity and support.

The footman led them up two flights and along the corridor halting outside a pair of double doors. He opened these and, still without a word being spoken, he bowed them into their new home. Emily sailed into the room. She waited until she heard the doors click shut behind them before releasing her breath. She stared, eyes wide and her mouth open.

'Look at this, girls; our sitting-room is bigger than the drawing room at Glebe House.'

'Do you think these rugs are Persian, Em? Are we allowed to walk on them?'

Emily laughed. 'Of course we are, you goose. They would not be on the floor otherwise.' The private sitting-room, with elegant *chaise-longues* and delicate gilt chairs was everything it should be. The two doors at the far end opened into a pair of matching bed chambers.

Serena ran forwards eager to explore. 'Can Millie and I share this one, Em? I love the rose-pink of the bed drapes. Do you see, it matches the curtains?'

Emily followed the girls around the room, exclaiming when expected, at the opulence of its appointments, but her mind was elsewhere, rehearsing what she would say and do when she met her future husband and her grandfather.

A discreet door, inset into the wood panelling, opened into a bathing closet and adjoining dressing rooms. Jenny was busy sorting out Emily's clothes. She curtsied. 'I'm almost finished, miss. Are you wishing to change your dress?'

Emily held up the torn skirt for inspection. 'I must. Is this ruined, or can you repair it?'

'I'm sure it will mend, Miss Emily. Now, Miss Amelia and Miss Serena, run along next-door. Mary's waiting for you.' She smiled as the girls looked round, puzzled.

'Where's the door, Jenny? I don't see one anywhere?'

'Go back into the bed chamber; you'll see another door, you go through there.'

Amelia stopped. 'Then we're not to sleep in here?'

'No, Miss Millie, this is Miss Emily's room. But yours is just as pretty, it's all done out in yellows and golds.'

It took Jenny half an hour to restore

Emily's appearance. Even her long chestnut brown hair was re-done and green ribbons, that matched her second new gown, were threaded through her hair.

'There, miss, you look a picture! Green suits you, and the combination you chose, of emerald silk for the under skirt and pale green muslin into the over dress, is perfect.'

'Thank you, Jenny. I'm still rather pale, but there's nothing I can do about that.' She turned sideways and her lips curled in a smile. 'I'm almost invisible from this view. It's fortunate that this new fashion pushes up one's chest; without that help I would look like a boy.'

'Go along with you, miss. You look lovely. No man in his right mind could ever mistake you for anything but a pretty young lady.'

The maid ran outside to alert the footman who was to escort her mistress downstairs. Emily brace herself for her ordeal. As Millie and Serena were to remain upstairs with Mary; she would have to brave the supercilious stares of the staff on her own. Jenny opened the door and the footman bowed.

'I am to take you to his lordship, Miss Gibson. Would you kindly follow me?'

Emily nodded and glided gracefully out of her sitting-room to retrace her steps down to the Grand Hall. She had time to wonder where her mother was and if her reunion with the Earl had progressed well, and then they were in front of imposing, ornately carved doors.

Two footmen guarded each side, like sentries. They sprang forward and flung open the double doors, leaving her framed in the doorway. One of them stepped forward and announced in a loud voice. 'Miss Emily Gibson, my lords.' He bowed and disappeared back down the wide carpeted passageway.

Emily felt unwelcome perspiration trickling down her spine as she walked into the room. The elderly gentleman, with a shock of grey hair, impeccably attired in superfine topcoat, knee breeches and shining top boots, watched his eldest granddaughter approach. He smiled, just. 'Welcome to Westerham, my dear. We are so glad you have found the time to join us, at last.'

Emily froze in mid-step and flags of colour appeared on her cheeks. She dropped into a low, formal curtsy, dipping her head, not wishing her anger to show. With careful elegance she rose and met the Earl of Westerham's critical gaze. 'I apologize if I kept you waiting, my lord.' She stopped there, offered no further explanation, or greeting, or effusion of delight at her incredible good fortune.

★   ★   ★

The man, leaning nonchalantly against the mantelshelf, his fair hair cut fashionably short, hid his smile. His great-grandfather would not like that answer one jot. Sebastian decided that maybe he had been premature in his judgement of Miss Gibson. The girl had backbone, and intelligence, and in that rig she looked almost presentable.

* * *

The Earl snorted. Emily ignored him, standing apparently relaxed, waiting for him to introduce her to Viscount Yardley. She dared not risk a glance in the direction of the intimidating gentleman she had noticed, observing her, aloof from the proceedings.

* * *

The Earl remembered his manners. 'My dear, allow me to present you to your cousin Sebastian, Viscount Yardley.'

Emily half turned and sank into a second graceful curtsy keeping her eyes down, as was expected of a well brought up young lady. To her surprise an elegant hand appeared and raised her to her feet. She looked up to meet the bluest eyes she had ever seen. They appeared to bore into her very soul. If he had not been holding her she would have taken an involuntary step backwards. Sebastian raised her gloved hand and pressed the back lightly with his lips. She was aware that although his mouth smiled his eyes were cautious, assessing her every move and, she believed, finding her wanting.

Incensed she snatched her hand back; it was a deliberate insult, but she was unable to help herself. If his expression had been unfriendly before, now it was arctic. His eyes narrowed and she could see him clench his teeth, obviously biting back a crushing set-down.

From somewhere she found the strength to speak. 'I am delighted to meet you, Cousin Sebastian.' Her cousin raked her from head to toe, dislike and disdain apparent in his every gesture.

'Are you indeed, cousin? I only wish I

could say the same.' He turned and half bowed to his great-grandfather. 'You will excuse me, I hope, sir?'

Without another word he sauntered out of the room leaving Emily so furious she forgot to be insulted. She glared after him, hating him, and for a glorious moment forgot that she had possibly just ruined her family's one chance of happiness.

4

'Well, my child, you certainly knocked him from his high horse.' The Earl chuckled, much amused by his granddaughter's spirited behaviour. Emily swung back to face him, her face crumpled and tears filling her eyes. 'I have offended him, my lord. He will never offer for me now.' The weight of failure was crushing her chest.

'Come and sit by me, my dear, and do not look so woebegone. If he does not want you, that will be his loss. There are plenty more eligible gentlemen out there for you to choose from, I can assure you. You are an heiress now.'

Her mouth fell open. 'But I thought I had to marry Viscount Yardley. I thought that was the arrangement between us.'

Her grandfather frowned. 'What arrangement, Emily? You wrote to me asking for my help in finding a husband; Sebastian is just the first suitable bachelor I have introduced you to.'

Emily sat down beside the old man. 'Are you saying that you do not mind if my cousin does not offer for me? You're not going to send us back?'

'Good God no! Of course not! Whatever gave you that ridiculous notion?'

Emily recalled the letter from the Earl. In it he had offered to find her a husband and suggested that Viscount Yardley might do; he had also offered to give them a permanent home. There had been no mention of sending them back. Her fevered imagination had manufactured the threat. She nodded, her eyes still damp.

'It appears I have misunderstood, my lord,' she said stiffly. 'But after the callous way you have treated my mother these past years, it is small wonder that I did so.'

He shifted on his chair and his lined

face flushed. 'You are right to take me to task, Emily, my dear. I have behaved abominably. I blamed my dear Althea for her mother's demise; I was so distraught at the time I was not thinking rationally.'

Emily was unimpressed. She regarded him sternly. 'But you also ignored my plea for help when our father died two years ago. Surely you were not still over-wrought at the loss of the countess then?'

He shook his head. 'I have no excuse, other than your appeal arrived on the anniversary of her death. It was not an auspicious time, as you can imagine, and opened old wounds.'

Emily jumped to her feet. She had heard enough of his feeble excuses. 'On my father's death you became the head of our household, my sisters and my legal guardian. You have shamefully shirked your responsibilities. If we were not in such desperate straits, believe me, sir, we would not be here now.'

Her grandfather pushed himself up out of his chair. He towered over her, his face thunderous. 'I shall not be taken to task by a chit of a girl; I am the Earl of Westerham and your grandfather and I expect to be treated with respect, at all times. Is that understood?'

She felt her courage desert her. She knew she had overstepped the mark and sincerely regretted her impertinence, however true her intemperate words had been she should have held her tongue. Then her spine stiffened and her head came up. She returned his glare, unbowed. 'I sincerely apologize for my incivility, my lord. You are quite right; I should never have spoken so rudely.' Her eyes flashed dangerously and her nostrils flared. 'However, I do not retract my words for they are the truth. I merely regret the way in which they were spoken.'

The Earl's face became redder and for a horrible moment Emily thought he would fall to the ground with an apoplexy. It was time to take her leave. She dropped a small curtsy and spun, her skirts flying out revealing her trim ankles, and walked briskly across the acres of polished boards and scattered rugs, praying she would reach the door before the explosion came. She did not.

'Come back here, miss. I have not finished with you yet.' The roared command bounced off the walls. She could not in all consciousness pretend she had not heard. She stopped, and slowly turned back to face him. He waited, stony faced, for her to retrace her steps.

She halted, two paces in front of him, keeping her eyes lowered, waiting for the torrent to break over her head. She heard him step forward and flinched, expecting to be felled by a blow. A gnarled, but surprisingly strong hand, reached out and gripped her chin, forcing her to look up.

'Well, my dear child, that was invigorating. I have not enjoyed myself so much for years.'

'I beg your pardon ... ' Emily stammered.

'I enjoy a good row — cleans the pipes — do you not agree? Come, Emily, do not look so worried. The show is over.' He laughed. 'You will have to get used to my temper if you wish to live here.' He released her chin and took her icy hand. 'You are trembling, child. I am sorry; I did not mean to frighten you. Come and sit with me.'

Emily allowed herself to be led to the settle by the fire, grateful for its reviving warmth. She was totally bemused. How could he change from terrifying to benevolent in a second? She regained her composure and dared to speak again. 'I don't understand. Are you no longer angry with me?'

He leant over and patted her hand. 'No, my dear, I am not. You enraged me for a moment; I shouted at you and then I felt better. It is always so for me. In time you will get used to it.'

'I'm not going to retract my words, sir. I do feel that you mistreated us this last two years.'

'I did, my dear. But I had no idea you were in such difficulties. Your letter merely stated that your father had died and that Althea was grieving and asked if I could help in anyway, did it not?' Emily nodded. 'However you did not tell me you were so strapped for cash that you could not pay the bills.' He scowled at the thought, causing her to recoil again.

She considered his explanation and found it to be true. 'I hoped you would send us help anyway, now that the reason for your disapproval had been removed.'

'I am sorry, my dear. You are quite right to admonish me; I should have offered to have you here then. I have sadly neglected my duties; can you find it in your heart to forgive an old man of five and eighty?'

'I suppose I must, sir. I would not wish a gentleman of your great age to meet his maker unforgiven.' Her words were bland but her eyes sparkled.

He chuckled. 'Thank you, my child.

Do you think you could call me grandfather now I am forgiven?'

She smiled, finding that she might actually be coming to like him. 'I can manage that, grandfather.' As matters were settled between them and they were in complete accord she felt emboldened to enquire after Lady Althea. 'Where is my mother, grandfather? Did your reunion not go well?'

'It went wonderfully. She forgave me and we embraced fondly.' He paused, his face concerned. 'Why she is so thin and poorly? I pray that she has not got the wasting sickness.'

'No. It's that after Papa's death she was unable to cope with the grief and fell ill. I believe she is like you in that respect. Her appetite all but vanished and I sincerely believe that without the doses of laudanum to give her release from her pain she would not still be with us.'

'She has grieved long enough. I know, I have wasted half my life doing the same. It is hoped the change of circumstances will start the healing process. She has retired to her rooms, the emotion of the occasion, plus the fatigue of the journey, have exhausted her.'

'I'm sure that she will start to recover here. She has been much more like herself ever since she received your letter. It has been a difficult two years, grandfather. I cannot tell you how glad I am to be here and to no longer have the responsibility of running Glebe House on my shoulders.'

The Earl sat back and studied her critically. He did not like what he saw. 'Are you ailing, too, Emily? You are stick thin, almost as wasted as my poor Althea.'

'No, grandfather, I'm as well as I could be. I'm sure now that I am here, I shall soon recover.'

'Are you telling me that your appearance is solely caused by lack of sustenance? That you have been unable to put enough food on the table?'

Emily blushed; it was not something

she was proud of. 'I made sure that Millie and Serena, and the staff, never went without, grandfather.'

'God dammit!' The Earl exploded, forgetting his manners in his anger. 'I shall never forgive myself for this, child. I promise I'll make it up to you. Never, never, will you want for anything again. My purse is deep and its contents are entirely at your disposal. Whatever you require, it is yours.'

'Do you mean that, grandfather? Anything at all?'

'Yes, of course. I do not make idle promises. What do you want? Name it?'

She sighed happily. 'I wish you to wave a magic wand so that I become so beautiful my obnoxious cousin falls under my spell and then I can turn him away with a broken heart. That is what I want.' She sat back, waiting for his laughter.

'Then that is what you shall have. With the right garments and decent food inside you we will turn you into the most beautiful girl in Surrey. And if you break that jackanapes' heart, it would do no more than serve him right.'

'Please, grandfather, I was only funning. I didn't mean it.'

'You did, my dear girl. I saw how he insulted you; you shall have your revenge. It's high time that young man was taught a lesson. He has had things his own way ever since he was in leading strings.'

Emily giggled, her wild idea now seemed a possibility. 'I put myself in your knowledgeable hands, grandfather. By the by, I do not really wish to be married at the moment. It was merely a ploy to gain some money for the family.'

'Excellent! I do not wish to lose you yet, my dear. I feel we are going to be the best of friends. We are two of a kind; you remind me of myself at your age.'

Neither of them mentioned that Sebastian was even more like his great-grandfather but they both thought it.

★   ★   ★

Emily decided to dine in her sitting-room, with the girls, that night. As she had no other dress, changing for dinner was an impossibility. Her mother was too exhausted, after all the excitement, and had retired to bed. She had no desire to eat on her own with her grandfather. Although cordial relations were now established, Emily was still finding it difficult to reconcile the two sides of the Earl of Westerham, irascible tyrant one moment and benevolent old gentleman the next. It was small wonder, she thought, Viscount Yardley had turned out so pompous.

Millie and Serena had gone off with Mary to explore their new home. They had already investigated the school rooms upstairs and found them admirable. Emily supposed a governess would have to be employed to continue their education. She intended to be far too busy learning how to be a polished lady of the *ton* instead of a country mouse.

Becoming bored with her book Emily

rang for Jenny. 'I'm going out for a walk; I wish to change into my brown walking dress and pelisse.'

'But that's so old, miss. You cannot wear such an outfit here.' Jenny was shocked to the core by such a suggestion.

'Fustian, Jenny. I have no other suitable for a long walk in the grounds. A mantua maker has been sent for from London but, until she arrives, and starts refurbishing our wardrobes, we must wear what we have, or stay shut up in our rooms all day.'

Stoutly shod in scuffed black half boots, an old chip straw bonnet rammed on her head, she was ready to venture out. Jenny was left behind. Emily did not consider that walking about the garden warranted a maid to accompany her.

A series of attentive young footmen sprung to attention at her footsteps and doors were opened and closed like clockwork. It was lucky that she, unlike most of her sex, had been blessed with good sense of direction and an excellent visual memory. She arrived in the Grand Hall without getting herself lost once. The frosty faced butler, Penfold, materialized beside her.

'Is Miss Gibson going outside, might I enquire?'

Emily almost looked round to see if *Miss Gibson* was accompanying her and was forced to cover her involuntary snigger by diving into her reticule. 'I am intending to take a walk around the park before it gets too dark.' She had to bite her tongue to stop herself from asking the self-important gentleman for permission to go out.

'Will Miss Gibson require an escort on her perambulations?'

'No, she will not.' Emily hurried to the front door and two footmen opened it with a flourish and bowed her through, like royalty.

She ran down the steps and her tinkling laughter was clearly heard by Sebastian, just returning from his ride, and about to take his magnificent chestnut stallion, Sultan, back to the stable yard. Instead he sent the horse skittering around the corner, scattering gravel and dirt, to investigate.

The sound of a horse approaching made Emily pause and she turned to face the noise. Judging by the stamping and the jangling, the animal approaching was large and spirited. Exactly the kind of horse she liked to ride herself.

Sultan danced, snorting, around the corner of the building, arriving at exactly the same time as she did. The horse, startled by her sudden appearance, half reared, and Sebastian swore loudly, expecting to have a fainting female collapse under his horse's massive hooves.

Emily laughed again, stepped sideways, and reached up to take the horse's bit. 'Steady, old fellow. Nothing to get so excited about.' She placed her free hand on the stallion's nose and brought it down to her level. 'You're a handsome boy, are you not?' She breathed, open mouthed into the horse's flaring nostrils, the odd action establishing an instant rapport with the normally savage beast.

Up to that point she had quite forgotten that the horse had not arrived alone. She had been so occupied making friends she had not heard his rider dismount.

'What the hell do you think you are doing? Do you want to be killed, you stupid girl?'

Emily found herself nose to nose with a furious man with blazing blue eyes. 'How dare you speak to me like that? I am not a serving maid.' They glared at each other, her huge hazel eyes glittered with righteous indignation.

Sultan, resenting the attention being taken from himself, lowered his head and nudged Emily firmly on the back. The unexpected push sent her flying into a solid wall of muscle. Sebastian, unprepared was unable to brace himself and he lost his balance and they tumbled backwards on to the ground.

The language he used was quite new to Emily. Her landing had been far softer than his; she was safely cradled in Viscount Yardley's arms, he had taken the full brunt of the hard ground. The situation was ridiculous and Emily laughed.

'I think, sir, that you should moderate your language; my ears are burning.'

Sebastian's swearing ceased instantly. He grinned, quite unrepentant, and suddenly looked much younger and less intimidating. 'And I think you, Miss Gibson, should consider your position; it is quite unseemly.'

At his words Emily immediately attempted to roll away but his arms tightened, holding her still. She could feel the heat flood from top to toe and hated her second cousin for causing her so much embarrassment.

'Please, release me, immediately. I wish to stand up.' Her voice was little more than a whisper and Sebastian realized, too late, that he had gone too far. This was no fast London debutante but a shy country girl.

With one lithe move he sat up, placing Emily on the ground beside him as he did so. Before she could attempt to stand he was up and taking her hands pulled her easily to her feet. He stepped back, his expression serious.

'I apologize, Miss Gibson; that was out of order. I treated you with disrespect and you do not deserve that.'

Emily glanced nervously upwards. What she saw reassured her. 'I accept your apology, sir. It appears that we are destined to fall out every time we meet'

He smiled, his eyes warm with amusement. 'Fall over, on this occasion, I think, Cousin Emily.'

Emily felt herself blush again, but this time it was for quite a different reason. To cover her disquiet she busied herself with the shaking out of her dress, glad she was not wearing either of her new gowns. When she had recovered her composure she answered, the tone as light as his.

'Let us hope our meetings in future are less hazardous, Cousin Sebastian.' For some reason she felt that her words might come to back to haunt her.

5

Lady Althea opened her eyes and for a moment was not sure where she was. She gazed round the delightful chamber, decorated in the Oriental style. On the bed hangings, and the curtains, dark red poppies and lush green leaves rioted, the colours nearly as fresh as the day they were hung almost thirty years ago.

With a sigh of pleasure she sank back into the pillows, she was home, sleeping in the rooms she had occupied until she had defied her parents and married Peter Gibson. She could remember clearly the day she and her mother had selected the exotic materials still hanging here.

For the first time in two long years she felt contented with her lot. She believed she was finally turning the corner and could start to live her life without the support of her beloved husband. Still smiling, she leant over and gently tugged the bell rope. She would rise and take a bath. Using the bathing room again after so long would be a novelty.

Edwards appeared beside her. 'Yes madam? Are you ready to rise?'

'I am, Edwards. But first I would like a bath. I do not intend to go down this evening so lay out an old gown, any will do.'

Her dresser beamed. 'The water is on its way. I heard you sit up and sent word down. There is a note come up for you, my lady, will you read it now?'

Lady Althea held out an elegant hand, the veins showing blue through her pale skin. She unfolded the paper and seeing the contents laughed out loud. A sound Edwards had not heard for far too long.

'Excellent! The Earl has arranged for Madame Ducray to come down from town bringing a selection of materials and ready sewed gowns, for us to choose from. She will be staying at

Westerham until all four of us have completely renewed our wardrobes. Is that not splendid news?'

Edwards nodded. 'Yes, madam. It's high time you all had new gowns.'

The sound of clattering buckets was clearly heard from the adjoining bathing room and Lady Althea got out of bed with enthusiasm.

'I think I shall have my hair washed as well, Edwards. Perhaps you should cut it for me; it has become far too long and straggly, has it not?'

Two hours later Lady Althea was resting comfortably in her sitting-room, her hair freshly styled and her navy blue eyes alert. She was awaiting a visit from her younger daughters. What had become of Emily, she had no idea. Edwards had sent a message with one of the chambermaids to her room but had found it unoccupied.

Serena and Millie were outside in the passageway and she smiled to think that now her precious girls would be able to grow up in the same luxurious surroundings as she had. If she had had any inkling of exactly what her normally sensible and sedate eldest daughter was doing, at that very moment, she would have been horrified.

★   ★   ★

Sultan stamped his huge hooves impatiently, he was eager to return to his cosy stable. Being ignored again, he snatched his bridle from his master's hand stretching his nose high into the air. It had the desired effect.

'Stand, sir. Enough of that nonsense,' Sebastian said, laughing at his mount's antics.

'I believe he's trying to tell you that he wishes to be in his stable, not standing about here.' Emily reached up and stroked the velvety nose. She was already in love with this horse. She would dearly love to ride him but knew her cousin would never agree to such a thing. But something prompted her to ask.

'Would you permit me to ride Sultan? He's similar to the stallion I was forced to sell after my father died.'

Sebastian's eyebrows shot up under his hair. 'Good God! Are you saying you have ridden such an animal yourself?'

Emily laughed, delighted she had surprised her cousin. 'Indeed I have; and I'm not ashamed to say that I always rode astride. I have a habit specially made for that purpose.'

'I do not believe it. No girl alive could ride a horse like Sultan safely.' She bristled and her smile vanished. How dare he call her a liar! Emily threw back her head and challenged him.

'Give me a leg up and you will see just how wrong you are.'

For a moment Sebastian hesitated; it was an outrageous suggestion. Then he saw the fury in her remarkable eyes and decided it would not hurt her to learn a sharp lesson. He would call her bluff.

'Very well; we will take him somewhere safer. The back paddock will do.'

He viewed her dusty old-fashioned dress as they walked towards the field. 'Do you need to change into your habit?'

She shook her head. 'No, this skirt is full enough; I shall manage.'

Sultan, on discovering he was not to be put into his box, began to show his displeasure by sidling and throwing his head about. Emily was beginning to regret her rash decision but she would not back down; she wished her cousin to discover that, unlike the usual debutantes, there was more to her than feminine fripperies and inane chatter.

It quite escaped her attention that so far, in their brief acquaintance, she had not shown the slightest sign of being either feminine or a chatterbox.

'Are you certain you wish to go through with this, cousin? I will quite understand if you feel you are not up to riding Sultan when he is in this mood.' If he had not accompanied the suggestion with a superior smile Emily might have agreed. In spite of her prowess as a horsewoman, she was starting to think that she would not be able to control the overexcited animal.

'No, definitely not. I have said I shall ride him and ride him I shall.' They had reached the three acre meadow in which the house cows and miscellaneous poultry lived. The gate latch was stiff and Sultan refused to stand still and allow Sebastian to open it. Without a second thought Emily stepped up and removed the bridle from her cousin's hand.

'Stop that, silly boy,' she murmured as she walked him in a small, tight circle. The horse was so surprised to be led by such a small human that he lowered his huge head and nuzzled her back. 'That's better; I don't understand what all the fuss is about.'

'The gate is open. Bring him in,' Sebastian snapped, annoyed that his horse was behaving like a donkey with his smug cousin.

Emily led Sultan into the field and

heard the gate clang with an unnecessarily loud bang behind her, making Sultan shy violently, lifting her off her feet for a second.

'It's all right, boy, it's only a silly gate. Slammed by a silly person. Calm down now.'

Sebastian almost snatched the reins back. 'You had better adjust the leathers to suit you. I shall hold him for you.'

She held the stirrup under her arm, the quickest way to judge the length she needed, and moved the buckle up five holes. She went round to alter the other and was then ready to mount. She knew Sebastian was expecting her to back down; she would not give him the satisfaction. She gathered up the reins. She could barely reach the horse's withers; she bent back her leg and felt Sebastian take it and then she was in the saddle and Sultan was her responsibility.

She settled herself more securely and slackened the reins, allowing Sultan to flex his neck, or had he so desired, to take hold of the bit and bolt off with her. She heard a sharp intake of breath beside her and knew her cousin was regretting his rash move and was about to step back and grab the bridle.

She clicked her tongue and squeezed her legs firmly and the horse moved away smoothly into a perfect, balanced trot. Emily relaxed; the handsome chestnut was a joy to ride, the most responsive mount she had ever had

She pushed him into a canter and took him in a figure of eight around the paddock. On the second circuit she asked him for a flying change and he obliged. She forgot everything in the exhilaration of the experience. She was unaware that she was showing an indecent amount of leg or that she had attracted a large audience of grooms and stable hands as word of her exploits had spread round the yard.

She rode Sultan for twenty minutes before deciding it was time to allow him to return to his box. After all, he had already been ridden hard by his owner all afternoon. She reined in smoothly at the gate, her face flushed and her eyes sparkling. It was only then she noticed the row of grinning faces lined up against the fence.

Good heavens, had the entire staff of Westerham come out to see her? She also became aware that her cousin was not sharing her pleasure. Sebastian was standing, arms folded, his full lips curled in supercilious disdain.

Her heart plummeted. Why had she allowed pride to push her into such a situation? She could feel the warm afternoon breeze cooling her bare calves and knew she had made a dreadful error of judgement. In the space of twenty short minutes she had destroyed her precious reputation. She had also brought disgrace to her mother and her grandfather.

Shamefaced, she did not wait for assistance to dismount. She swung her leg over the saddle and dropped expertly to the ground. She patted Sultan's neck — after all, it was not his fault she had made an exhibition of herself — and, outwardly calm, she handed his reins to a waiting groom.

Without bothering to speak she turned and walked through the open gate, and head held high, the sun glinting on her russet hair, she stalked, apparently unconcerned, back to the house.

Once inside she flew up the stairs and ran along the passageways. It was far too late to worry about scandalizing the staff with such immodest behaviour. Her sitting room was mercifully empty; at least her sisters were not there to witness her humiliation. She found her maid in the box room that was now her own.

'Jenny, can you prepare me a hot bath. I shall not get dressed again. I'm going to retire. I have a severe megrim.'

Her abigail wisely refrained from commenting on the fact that her mistress smelled strongly of horse and her once clean dress was now liberally covered with chestnut hair. Nor did she remind Emily that it was her sister Amelia who normally suffered from sick headaches, not her.

Somewhat restored by her total immersion in warm water, Emily retired to her imposing, old-fashioned, four-poster bed, and firmly pulled the heavy damask curtains around her. She had always considered such beds as suitable only for elderly folk but that afternoon she was grateful she could hide in the privacy the drapes created.

In the pink gloom, little sunlight filtering through the heavy material, she sat and considered her position. She had been at Westerham scarcely a day and had already managed to offend just about everyone she had met. She had vomited in the bushes in front of Mr Foster, caused her grandfather to lose his temper and offended her extremely high in the instep Cousin Sebastian, not once but twice.

It was a good thing she no longer had to persuade him to marry her. She would never forget the look of absolute disgust on his face as he leant casually against the paddock fence. It would be forever etched on her mind. She did not care that he held her in dislike for her opinion of him was equally dismal.

However the good opinion of both her mother and grandfather were quite a different matter. Her behaviour would have been considered unacceptable even for Millie. And as she was still legally under the control of the earl, he could administer whatever punishment he felt she deserved. If it had been Amelia at fault she supposed he could order a sound spanking, but she was reasonably sure she would be considered too old to receive such treatment.

Slowly her lips curled in a rueful smile. She was actually disciplining herself. After all she had put herself to bed at five o'clock in the afternoon without any supper, had she not? As her empty stomach grumbled alarmingly, she realized it was going to be a very long and uncomfortable time until breakfast.

Emily stretched out her aching limbs, for it had been so long since she had last ridden her body was protesting, and settled down. Her only recourse was to try and sleep the hours away. Unfortunately her dreams were not happy. She spent the entire night being pursued by irate persons of varying ages and sizes but all of them, without exception, possessed a pair of startlingly blue eyes.

Sebastian watched Emily walk away and, in spite of his disgust at her total disregard for the acceptable proprieties, he felt a small measure of admiration at her courage. He pushed himself away from the fence and, ignoring the speculative stares of the staff, strolled off in the direction of the house. He found himself grinning as he pictured his cousin riding his horse so superbly; he was forced to admit that he had never seen a better female rider and neither were there many men who could manage a spirited stallion like Sultan the way she had.

He had accepted her inappropriate challenge expecting her to renege, giving him the welcome opportunity to administer a sharp set-down. If he had thought for a moment that she actually intended to ride, astride, in her walking dress, he would never have agreed. Now she had disgraced herself in front of half the outside staff. A lady would never have exposed herself to such ridicule, even to prove a point.

He shuddered to think what the earl would say when he heard, as inevitably he would, about her exploits. And the wretched girl's poor mother, what of her? She was obviously unwell; would her daughter's unpardonable behaviour cause Lady Althea to suffer a relapse?

He stopped. It was as though someone had thrown an icy bucket of water over his head. How could he be castigating his cousin when the entire episode was entirely his fault? She could not have ridden if he had not only agreed, but actively given her the assistance she needed to mount.

He felt his face suffuse with unaccustomed shame. What had come over him? He was a diplomat, renowned for his level headedness and sharp intellect, but he had allowed himself to be drawn into an appalling escapade solely because his pride had been dented.

He swore, vilely, to himself, and lashed out at a nearby pedestal upon which a shiny marble cherub rested. The agonizing pain that shot up his foot was enough to bring him to his senses. It was his fault. He had somehow to make amends. He was a gentleman and he could not allow his cousin to be blamed for something that was his responsibility. For her to lose her good name would be intolerable, he could see that now. But how he was to save her from certain ruin he had not the slightest notion.

The earl explained to him his only course of action, in no uncertain terms. 'Good God, boy, this is a disaster! It is of your making, what were you thinking of? Word of Emily's exploits will be all over the county by morning. Your stupid behaviour has ruined the reputation of an unspoiled country miss. She did not know that what she proposed would destroy her. You certainly did.'

Sebastian almost hung his head. He had not felt so wretched since he was a schoolboy and been reprimanded for a childish prank. How was it possible that a dowdy, beanpole of a chit, had caused him to behave so badly when enraged Prussian generals had failed to move him?

'I accept full responsibility for the incident, sir. It should never have happened. I know that. It was inexcusable of me to allow my cousin to ride astride, in public, improperly dressed.'

His great-grandfather snorted. 'Are you trying to imply, sir, that if she had been wearing a habit and ridden in private that such a display would have been acceptable?'

'No, of course I am not. I just meant . . . ' he stopped, there was nothing to say. He was guilty as charged and ready to do whatever it took to put things right. If Sebastian had seen his grandfather's satisfied smile whilst he was staring morosely at his boots, he might have been more alert. Might have reacted more quickly, been able to extricate himself from the trap.

'And I have your word that you are prepared to do whatever it takes to remedy the situation?'

'Yes, sir, you have.'

'Very well; you have no alternative, you must offer for Emily. The only way her reputation can be salvaged is by becoming your fiancée. People will forgive what takes place between a betrothed couple, however outlandish it might be.'

Sebastian's head shot up, his eyes wide, his complexion white. He met the implacable stare and knew he had no choice. 'I agree, my lord. I will offer for her tomorrow.'

'Well done, my boy; you have made the right decision.' The Earl of Wester-ham left, chuckling happily, leaving the prospective bridegroom sitting, head in his hands, in total misery. It was not just Emily's life that had been ruined by his stupidity, he had also ruined his own.

6

The late September sun poured through the window bathing the room in golden light. Emily didn't notice. She was preparing herself to brave the outside world, to face the inevitable sniggers and sneers from the hundreds of Westerham staff who knew, even better than its occupants, exactly how a lady should behave.

The mantle clock struck eight. Was it too early to venture down in search of sustenance? She hoped she would feel more confident when her hunger was satisfied, but she doubted it.

'Jenny, do you think there is any food put out in the breakfast parlour?'

'Shall I go down and find out, miss? You don't want to have a wasted journey.'

Whilst she waited for her maid's return Emily paced the room quite unaware of what an attractive picture she presented. Her normally pale cheeks were prettily flushed, her eyes sparkled and the sun shone in her russet hair. But although the small waist and flowing skirt of her sage green dress flattered her, even to the most partial of viewers, she was over thin. The front of her bodice was little fuller than the back.

'They are putting out the chafing dishes now, miss. His lordship likes to break his fast early, I am told.'

'Thank you, Jenny. I will go down. I have to face him sometime, I suppose.'

★　★　★

A footman sprung to attention at her approach, barely hiding his smile. He opened the parlour door with an exaggerated flourish and showed her in.

★　★　★

The room was not empty. Viscount Yardley was at that very moment piling his plate high with a mixture of sliced ham, coddled eggs and field mushrooms. He had had little sleep and his face was drawn and grey. When he heard the door open he looked up, his expression irritated. This instantly changed to absolute horror when he saw who had interrupted him. Was there to be no respite? Surely a condemned man could be allowed to eat his last meal in peace?

★ ★ ★

Emily saw his expression and instantly her hackles rose. In her long, mostly sleepless, night she had come to the same conclusion as her grandfather. She would not be in this mess if it was not for the man staring so rudely at her. She was tempted to retreat and leave him to eat his meal in peace but she was famished and, however disagreeable her cousin, she was not going to leave the room without filling her empty stomach.

Sebastian nodded, his brimming plate still in his hand, and Emily nodded back. She knew the correct etiquette was for a lady to be seated and the gentleman to wait on her. Should she sit or help herself? Her stomach gurgled alarmingly and made the decision for her.

The plates were still warm and the food smelt appetizing. Ladies didn't pile their plates but Emily didn't care; she had been half starved for the last two years and now her body craved nourishment. Ignoring her cousin she put a random selection of hot food on her plate and took it to the far end of the long dining table. Then she returned for several slices of hot toast and a large pat of freshly churned butter.

She heard what sounded suspiciously like a snort of laughter, quickly repressed, and glanced up. Sebastian was having difficulty containing his mirth.

'Is there anything else I can get you

Cousin Emily? You appear to have missed out on the cold cuts and muffins.'

Emily tried to swallow her retort but it burst out of its own volition. 'If you had spent the past two years living on as little as I have you would also wish to fill your plate.'

This unexpected answer caused him to swear. 'Dammit, Emily, are you telling me your situation has been so dire that there was not enough food on your table?'

'Yes, that is exactly what I am telling you, sir. What little there was went to my sisters and mother first, I made do with what was left.'

He shook his head; for a moment unable to think of something appropriate to say. 'I am sorry to hear that, my dear. It is almost unbelievable that your family has been in such poor circumstances when your grandfather could have provided you with everything you needed.'

Emily dived into her breakfast too hungry to answer. Only when the plate was half empty did she pause and look up. She found, to her astonishment, that instead of seeing a pair of critical blue eyes staring back at her she was on her own. Viscount Yardley had vanished. She had been so engrossed in her excellent repast, she had not heard him depart. His breakfast remained, untouched, on the buffet.

She sighed, exasperated that her Cousin Sebastian was so finicky he could not bear to see a lady eat as heartily as she did. For the second time in twenty-four hours she congratulated herself on a lucky escape; being married to such a stickler would be tedious in the extreme.

★   ★   ★

Sebastian watched his young cousin devouring her food and instead of being revolted he was angry, furiously angry. Now he knew that her pallor and extreme thinness was caused by semi-starvation, he could see that within a few weeks Emily would be a lovely young woman. In fact she would be a diamond of the first water.

His march through the house had taken him to the earl's apartments. The footman knocked at the door and announced him.

'Good heavens, my boy, this is an early visit. What has brought you here in such a pucker?'

Sebastian gestured impatiently for the footman to leave them before he spoke. His voice was controlled but his fury quite apparent.

'How can you accuse me of ruining Emily's life, sir, when you have allowed the poor girl to slowly starve these past two years? It is unpardonable. If you were a younger man I would call you out.'

The Earl recoiled and grasped a chair-back for support. He appeared to crumble and suddenly he was no longer a wealthy, powerful aristocrat but a vulnerable old man. Sebastian realized, too late, he had allowed his anger at

Emily's treatment to overcome his common sense. What sort of diplomat was he? Why he was behaving like a veritable greenhorn he had no idea. A stripling straight from school would have better manners.

Instantly remorseful his anger evaporated. 'I am sorry, grandfather; I did not mean to distress you.' He came forward and helped the old man to a chair, waiting until he was seated and comfortable before he spoke again. 'Emily's half starved; how could you have allowed this to happen?' His enquiry was mild this time.

The old man shrugged. 'I did not know how bad things were. I know that is no excuse but I intend to make amends for it now. Those girls will want for nothing, I promise you. I want to give Emily a season, if that is what she would like.'

Sebastian could sense a reprieve. If Emily went to London, it was possible she would meet someone more to her liking. She had made it patently obvious that she held him in little regard.

'That sounds like an excellent idea, sir'

'I am glad you approve, my boy.' He had now recovered his composure and was once more in control. 'As your fiancée she will have entrée to all the best homes. A young lady needs to see the world a little before settling down.'

'I have not asked her yet, grandfather. Have you considered the very real possibility that she will refuse me? We do not suit you know.'

'Stuff and nonsense! Emily will do as she is bid, once things have been explained to her.' He paused, lost in thought. 'I will speak to her after I have broken my fast. Then you *will* make her an offer. I expect you to appear at eleven o'clock sharp, in the library, is that understood?'

'Yes, sir. I shall be there.' He had no option, he had given his word and he was now obliged to ask a most unsuitable girl to be his wife. He shuddered as he considered the mayhem she could cause in the refined world of international diplomacy. But he had promised. He was obliged to marry her unless she could be persuaded to cry off. His mobile mouth slowly curled at the corners. What if he made himself so objectionable Emily decided that his wealth and title would not compensate her for being shackled to him? Sebastian bowed.

'If you will excuse me, sir, I will speak to you later, when all is settled between my cousin and I.'

'See that you do.'

★   ★   ★

Emily swallowed the last two morsels of ham and placed her cutlery on her plate. She pushed back her chair and looked longingly at the remaining food still spread out on the sideboard. Did she have room, perhaps, for a hot muffin with bramble jelly?

★   ★   ★

The door opened and her grandfather was bowed in. Immediately she curtsied, dropping her eyes politely.

'Good morning, sir.'

'Good morning, my dear Emily. Please do not rush off; you can keep me company. Will you take a dish of tea whilst I break my fast?'

Emily straightened, her eyes widening. Whatever she had been expecting it was not such a convivial greeting. 'I would love to, thank you,' she added with a smile, 'I can highly recommend the ham and coddled eggs and the muffins look delicious also.'

He chuckled, his faded blue eyes almost disappearing in the creases. 'You may serve me, child, with whatever you enjoyed yourself. I have a devil of a job deciding.'

The footman retreated once the earl was safely seated. Happily Emily selected a variety of tempting items, but did not overfill the plate. She felt sure that an elderly gentleman would not wish to consume the same amount of food she had managed. He appeared satisfied with her choices and commenced his meal whilst she fetched him a mug of porter and poured tea into a delicate porcelain cup for herself.

She could delay no more; she would have to take the chair beside him. He allowed her to settle before he spoke. 'What were you thinking of child? Your display yesterday is the talk of Westerham and by this evening will be the topic of conversation in every house in the neighbourhood.' Emily had expected him to rant and rave and this quiet enquiry made her blush with shame.

'I am sorry, my lord. I was provoked. I know that is no excuse, but it could not have happened without Viscount Yardley's assistance. He is more culpable than me. It is to him you should apportion blame. I thought he was a diplomat. Is he not supposed to know how to behave in all circumstances?'

'Exactly, my dear girl. Yardley accepts the fault was his, even if the actions were yours. He is ready to take the necessary steps to save your reputation.'

'I do not understand. How can he do anything? It's too late, the damage is done.' Emily choked back a sob. 'Mama will be destroyed by this. She had such high hopes for me, and I shall never be received in society now, shall I?'

'You will, if you accept Yardley's offer.'

'His offer . . . ' she stammered. 'Are you saying I must marry him in order to put things right?' She gazed at her grandfather; her eyes widened and the colour left her face. 'Surely not? There has to be another way. I have no more wish to marry Viscount Yardley than he has to marry me.'

'Nonsense! You will deal admirably together. If you do not accept it will not just be your good name that will be lost. His will be gone also. Do you wish to ruin him as well as yourself?'

'Of course not.' She hung her head. Whatever she decided, her moment of foolishness was going to cause a lifetime's misery. She had no choice, but at least this way her sisters, her mother and her grandfather would be happy. After all, only yesterday she had been contemplating marriage to Sebastian as the solution to her family's problems. Her position now was no different, really.

She raised her head and pulled back her shoulders. Nobody would ever know how she felt about the situation.

'I shall accept Viscount Yardley's offer, when he makes one. I shall be honoured to become his betrothed, whatever the circumstances that promoted it.' Her smile was pitiful but he beamed back, delighted he had achieved his objective so soon.

'Good girl. You will not regret it. Sebastian can be a little stiff necked but never doubt his intelligence and his good heart.' He wiped his mouth on his starched white napkin. 'Now, run along, my dear. I am sure you wish to see your mother and deliver your good news. I expect you to be in the library at eleven o'clock sharp.' Still smiling brightly Emily rose gracefully to her feet, curtsied, and went, not to see her mother as suggested, but back to her room to find the privacy she craved.

Jenny was in the dressing-room mending her torn dress. 'I'm going to ride. Please find my habit right away.'

Less than fifteen minutes later Emily had escaped outside and was hurrying, head down, towards the stables. Sebastian was going the same way but from the rear of the house. He had been striding round the garden perfecting his plan.

Emily walked straight into him. Instinctively he closed his arms around her, protecting her from harm. The impact of their collision caused him to stagger backwards into the thick yew hedge that bordered the path. Its bulk prevented a second fall.

'Good grief, Emily! You almost had us over,' Sebastian said, as he carefully straightened and replaced her feet on the path.

'I beg your pardon; I was not looking where I was going. I hope I did not harm you?' Her voice was high and strained. She tried to smile and relax her rigid pose. 'I am hoping to find a mount; do you think there is one suitable for me?'

He stepped back, brushing the leaves and debris from his person. 'As long as you do not wish to ride Sultan, as I am about to go out myself. Will you accompany me? I can show you the estate, if you wish to see it?'

Emily took the olive branch. 'I would love to, thank you, Cousin Sebastian. And I can assure you I might be impulsive but I'm not stupid. I have no intention of setting tongues wagging a second time.'

'I am glad to hear it.' He offered her his arm and she felt it would be uncivil to refuse. The moment her hand rested on the rough fabric of his riding jacket she knew it to have been a mistake. She felt his muscles bunch beneath her light hold and believed that his reaction demonstrated his antipathy to her touch. She could not have been more wrong.

The progress had been noted by an observant stable boy and Sultan, and a spirited grey mare, were saddled and waiting when they arrived in the yard. Emily looked around with approval. The well-swept cobbles, freshly painted boxes and the glossy, enquiring heads hanging over half doors, told her that this was a well-kept stable yard.

Then she saw the horses standing ready and her smile, for the first time that morning, became genuine. Without pausing she stepped up to the huge chestnut stallion and rubbed his nose. He lowered his head to allow her to pull his ears.

'Good morning, you handsome fellow. How are you today?' The animal whickered and lipped her face with his whiskered mouth. 'Silly thing; you're too big for kisses.' As she stepped away she became aware that she was, once more, the centre of a circle of interested spectators. Her eyes met Sebastian's, they were not censorious, but amused. 'I'm sorry; but I could not resist greeting him.'

Grinning he leant down and with a pocket handkerchief wiped away the trail of slobber his horse had left on her forehead. 'There is no need to apologise; Sultan is sorely in need of friends. He is cordially disliked by all the grooms and lads who attend to him. For some strange reason he has fallen under your spell, Cousin.'

'You are bamming me? Sultan is not wild, he's a gentle giant.'

'I think his stable lad would dispute that, my dear.' He smiled; his eyes alight with laughter, making him suddenly look approachable and less severe. 'Do you like Polly, your mount? She is a fast ride but I am certain that you will have no difficulty handling her, even riding side-saddle.'

Emily turned her attention to the mare, who was more interested in flirting with the stallion. 'I love her. If I can not have Sultan for my own, I shall happily settle for Polly.'

The head groom threw her up into the saddle and she hooked one leg round the raised pommel. The other groom fitted her neatly booted foot into the single stirrup.

Sebastian vaulted into his saddle unaided and gathered up his reins. 'I thought we would take the route through Home Woods, there are hedges, logs and ditches to jump, and then come back across the park.'

'That sounds perfect. It's so long since I've been able to ride and I have missed it dreadfully.'

They clattered out of the yard in easy conversation. He had quite forgotten his vow to alienate his future wife by his obnoxious behaviour. She had quite forgotten that she disliked him. The dreaded appointment in the library was temporarily pushed aside by the exhilaration of the ride.

They arrived back two hours later, hot and mud-spattered, having spent the entire time without speaking a cross word. They parted, amicably, and when they returned to their apartments to change their garments neither of them gave a thought to what faced them in the library.

★ ★ ★

Sebastian dressed in a coat from Westons, cut square at the front as the newest fashion dictated. It took his man, Morrison, twenty minutes to ease him into this and his skin tight inexpressibles and highly polished Hessians. He tied his own neck cloth in an intricate arrangement he had devised for himself. Satisfied, he strode from his chamber, his jaw clenched and his expression grim.

He was faced with the prospect of spending the rest of his life in the company of someone he scarcely knew. It was a recipe for disaster. Then his expression relaxed a little as he recalled the pleasant two hours he had just spent in her company. He now considered that his plan to trick Emily into breaking the engagement was reprehensible and hardly appropriate to a man of his elevated position and he decided he had no option but to abandon it.

★ ★ ★

'I have repaired your lilac gown, miss; it's all ready for you, and I took the liberty of calling up a bath.'

'Thank you, Jenny. I will not wear that dress, an older one will suffice.' For a moment she was puzzled by her maid's look of horror at the suggestion. Then she felt as though she had swallowed a stone. For in less than an hour she was supposed to be in the library ready to agree to marry her cousin.

It was so unfair! She had been given her life back by her grandfather and had thrown it all away by a moment of foolhardiness. She knew she had no choice. She couldn't understand why the prospect of marrying her cousin filled her with such dread. After all he was handsome, intelligent, wealthy and titled. Most debutantes would love to be in her position. Why was she so set against the match?

7

The harsh sound of a clock striking the hour made Emily jump. She was late. How could that have happened? She quickened her steps, lifted her skirt, and ran lightly downstairs. Where was the library? The vast hall was deserted, and none of the usual footmen in sight. There were five routes for her to select from but she had no idea which one to take.

Frantically she searched for a bell-cord in order to summon assistance but found none. Then she had an inspired notion; she would open the front door and knock loudly on it; that would surely bring Penfold out of hiding.

Pleased with her scheme she turned the heavy knob and stepped out into the morning sunshine. The trees were so lovely in their autumn colours that she became distracted and released her hold on the door. Its swung shut with an ominous clunk. She spun round too late, the door was firmly closed. She lifted the heavy brass knocker and banged it. She waited expectantly. There was no sound of footsteps hurrying to her summons. She banged again, with such force that she hurt her hand. Yesterday the wretched place had been overrun with staff, where were they all today?

She decided to abandon the front door and search for another entrance. Penfold, who had been closeted with Mrs Todd, the housekeeper, opened the door to see a flash of lilac vanish round the corner. It was not his place to question the strange ways of his betters, so he quietly shut the door and went about his business.

Emily was breathless, and the hem of her dress limp and dusty by the time she finally found a side door that opened. She burst in, startling two parlour maids about their duties.

'Thank Heavens! I have found

someone. Please could you direct me to the library?'

The younger girl recovered first. 'Yes, miss, if you would care to follow me.'

Emily was late, very late. Her hair was escaping from its pins and the hem of her dress was mired but in her urgency she failed to notice.

★   ★   ★

Sebastian was glaring out across the park; he did not like to be kept waiting. The sound of her hurrying footsteps alerted him. He turned, and stood, legs slightly apart, arms rigidly beside him, and waited.

'Miss Gibson, my lord.' The maid, duty done, disappeared but not before she had noted the Viscount's expression and Emily's appearance. Both would be described in detail to the rest of the staff when they sat down for supper that night.

Emily curtsied and as her eyes dropped she saw the appalling state of her dress. Her spirits sunk even lower. This was not an auspicious start. She raised her head and shrivelled under the icy stare of her future husband. Where was the friendly man she had just been out riding with?

There was an interminable silence; Emily did not speak, she felt too ill. Sebastian knew if he opened his mouth too soon he would say something they would both regret.

Emily recovered her composure. 'I must apologize for keeping you waiting, sir.' She was about to explain why she was late but he forestalled her. She noticed that there appeared to be something wrong with his breathing.

'For God's sake, sit down, Emily and let us get this farce completed.'

Every instinct told her to flee from this formidable man but her feet refused to move. He took a step towards her and fearing that he was going to strike her, she retreated until her shaking back was hard against the door, her eyes wide.

'Please, I'm sorry. I got locked out.' To her shame she felt unwanted tears spill out and trickle down her cheeks.

'It is I who must apologize, Emily.' Sebastian took her hand and gently drew her towards a sofa. 'Sit down, my dear, you are shaking. I should not have frightened you like that; it was inexcusable. I am behaving like a nincompoop. Here, use this.' Emily felt the soft touch of a linen handkerchief placed into her fingers and obediently wiped eyes.

'I am not usually a watering-pot. I don't understand what's happening to me. I promise you, I am usually a woman of good sense.'

'It is this wretched business. It has got to us both, has it not?'

She nodded. 'You have no more wish for this than I do, do you, Cousin Sebastian?'

'No, I do not. But I am afraid we have no choice, my dear. Our behaviour yesterday has put us beyond the pale and only the announcement of our engagement will save us both from ruin.'

'Grandfather told me you could lose your position in the government as well as in society. Is that truly the case?'

'It is; we have no choice.' Then he smiled and inexplicably her heart turned over. He reached over and took her hand. 'Miss Gibson, will you do me the inestimable honour of becoming my wife?'

She swallowed twice, before answering. There appeared to be a lump stuck in her throat. 'Yes, my lord, I will.' The pull on her hand continued and she found herself being embraced by two exceptionally well-muscled arms.

'Look at me, Emily,' he commanded. She did as she was bid and received her first adult kiss. The feel of another mouth on hers was at first alarming but slowly she relaxed and began to enjoy the strange sensation.

'There, it is done.' Viscount Yardley released her and stood up. 'I assume you will tell Lady Althea our good news?'

'Yes, of course I will. What happens

next? Are we obliged to do anything else?'

'No; I am returning to Town after I have spoken to the Earl.' He bowed formally and, without further conversation, strode out of the room.

Emily stared at the closed-door scarcely able to comprehend what had just taken place. In the space of thirty minutes she had been shouted out, scared half to death, comforted, proposed to, kissed and abandoned. It was too much to take in. Shakily she got to her feet and began to walk around the room, trying to bring order to her tumbled thoughts.

She was still in the library when her sister discovered her. Millie greeted her with a scream of delight.

'Em, here you are! I have been searching for you for hours. Everything is like a game of hide and go seek in this huge house.'

Emily put down her book and returned her sister's happy smile. 'I know, Millie, I got lost this morning and have not dared venture out of here again. Is there a particular reason you are seeking me?'

'Yes, Madame Ducray from London has arrived and has boxes of samples and things to show you. Mama has got dressed and taken some breakfast. I love Westerham; we're going to be so happy here.'

'I'm sure you're right. Come along then, shall we try and find Mama's apartments or ring for assistance?'

'We had better ring; she will be getting anxious.'

Lady Althea greeted her daughters as though they had been lost for weeks. 'My dears, at last, I have been so worried. Where ever have you been for so long?'

'Em was hiding in the library; it took me for ever to find her.'

'Well you are both here now. Madame Ducray has set up in your sitting-room, Emily. She is waiting to see us there.'

Serena bounced off the *chaise-longue*.

'Shall there be dresses for me as well, Mama?'

'Of course, my love. Your grandfather said we are to have whatever we wish. He has placed no restrictions on expenditure.'

It was only then that Emily realized her mother and sisters were ignorant of either her scandalous behaviour or her precipitate engagement.

'Mama, I have to speak with you first. Millie, take Serena into Madame and tell her that we shall be along in a few minutes.'

'Can we start choosing material for our dresses and pinafores?'

Lady Althea answered. 'Yes you can, my dears. Madame will direct your attention to those most suitable for girls of your age.'

Mary led her charges away leaving Emily and her mother alone. 'You have not heard what happened yesterday, have you Mama?'

'I heard that you and Papa fell out but were reconciled immediately. I also heard that Viscount Yardley and you were at daggers drawn. Surely there can not be anything else?'

'I'm afraid there is. You had better sit down whilst I tell you.'

When Emily finished her story her mother was shocked speechless, but only for a moment.

'Am I to understand that you are now engaged to be married to Viscount Yardley and he has departed for Town without bothering to speak to me?'

Emily nodded. 'He asked grand-father's permission to address me. I suppose he felt that was sufficient.'

Lady Althea was incensed. She knew she had been slighted and did not take it kindly. 'I think it is the outside of enough. I have known of his existence scarcely a day and already I cordially dislike him. You shall not marry him, Emily, I will not have it.'

'But if I do not, both of us will lose our reputations. The scandal will also reflect on both you and the girls. I cannot allow that to happen.'

Her mother pursed her lips then her eyes lit up. 'I have it, Emily. When we have replenished our wardrobes, we shall go to Town. Although it is not high Season there will still be plenty going on. We can be ready in a month or less. I shall write at once to all my old acquaintances and get invitations for us to the most prestigious dances and soirées. As Viscount Yardley's fiancée, and my daughter, you will be accepted everywhere.'

Emily interrupted her mother's excited plans. 'But why? How will that help?'

'It is as plain as the nose on your face, my love. You will be considered a success, your reputation will be restored and then you can break the engagement and no one will think twice about it.'

'What reason shall I give for doing so? I don't wish to be called a jilt on top of everything else.'

'We shall just say you do not suit after all. I will think of something. Papa has promised to make all of you a generous settlement. You are now an heiress. There will be no shortage of eligible suitors, I can assure you.'

Emily did not point out that she really had no desire to be married to anyone. It seemed a shame to dampen her mother's enthusiasm. It was so long since she had seen her taking an interest in anything.

'Is there no way that Viscount Yardley could cry off without damaging his name?'

'No, my love. The man is honour bound to keep his promise, but society understands that it is a woman's privilege to change her mind.' Lady Althea rose. 'Come, Madame will think us discourteous if we do not appear.'

★　★　★

Emily's sitting-room had been transformed into an Indian bazaar. Silks, satins, sarcenet and muslins exploded over chair backs and sofas, cascading into pools of liquid colour on the polished boards. Upon the occasional tables were spread pages from *La Belle Assemblée*, with the latest fashion plates for adults and children alike.

The petite Frenchwoman, her brindled hair scraped back into an unflattering bun, fluttered forward, her tiny hands waving theatrically. 'Oh, Lady Althea, Miss Gibson, we are so 'appy to see you 'ere. I 'ave some lovely gowns made up for you to wear whilst I am constructing your new choices.'

Madame ushered her clients to the one uncluttered sofa. 'If you will please to sit 'ere, I will 'ave my girls show you the gowns that are complete.' Emily and Lady Althea sat where directed. There was no sign of either Millie or Serena.

'Where are my girls, Madame? Surely they have not become bored so quickly?'

'Oh no, my lady. They are in the chamber with their nurse, trying on the new clothes with great enthusiasm. Are you ready? I will call my assistants to begin.'

'Can I really select as many outfits as I wish, Mama? Does grandfather have bottomless pockets?'

Lady Althea patted her daughter's hand. 'He is one of the warmest men in England, my love, so do not stint yourself. I promise you that I have no intention of doing so. I never thought to have a closet bursting with lovely gowns ever again. I believed that I had forgone such luxuries when I married your dear Papa.'

Emily tensed, waiting for the torrent of tears that always followed such a mention but it didn't come. She smiled.

'I'm certain that he would want you to look beautiful again. Indeed, you're looking better already. I'm sure that in a few weeks you will be feeling fully restored and well enough to travel to London with me.'

'I shall, my love, I shall.' Lady Althea stared intensely at her eldest daughter. 'You are also far too thin, my love. We must both endeavour to eat more.

Slender is attractive but stick thin, I am afraid, is not.'

Emily giggled. 'If I continue to eat as I did this morning I will be the size of a horse in no time'

Madame coughed politely, drawing their attention to the entrance of the first of the two mannequins. After two hours even the delight of selecting new gowns was beginning to pall for all the company. They decided to postpone the measuring and fitting for the afternoon.

Lady Althea returned to her rooms promising she would eat before resting. Emily and her sisters found their way back downstairs to the small dining parlour where, they had been informed, a cold collation had been set up for them.

'I have four new dresses, with matching slippers, and bonnets and ribbons as well,' Serena told Emily proudly.

'And I have the same. How many did you select Em?' Millie asked.

'I am now the proud possessor of two

morning gowns, two tea dresses, one walking dress with matching pelisse, and one evening gown. I have, naturally, a full complement of slippers, bonnets, reticules and shawls to accompany them. I shall be so smart you will not know me.'

'Mary says we are having lots of other garments made especially. I do not see when we will have time to wear them all. And I expect I will have grown out of them before they are even half worn out.'

'You have to change your outfit every hour, Serena; it is what happens in the *ton*, is it not, Em?' Serena looked suitably horrified.

'Do not tease your sister, Millie. No, Serena, you do not have to change so often. However, I believe that it is not done to wear the same dress twice in public, but that only applies to adults I am sure.'

The girls stared, open-mouthed. Millie was the first to recover. 'But that can not be right. It would mean having hundreds of dresses; no one would have so many. It would be too wasteful.'

'Three hundred and sixty five dresses, if you went out every day,' Serena said with awe. 'No wonder we have such enormous closets in our chambers.'

Emily shook her head laughing openly at her sisters. 'Don't take me so literally, girls. By 'out in public' I meant to a party, ball, or soirée, not walking or driving in the park.'

By the end of the day the Gibson family was exhausted, but they were all well satisfied by the day's events. Madame Ducray was even more so, for she returned to London with an order of such magnitude she would be obliged to take on more seamstresses if it was to be completed on time. It had been arranged that she would deliver the finished items to Westerham within four weeks, in order that any alterations could be made before the party departed for London.

★   ★   ★

The Earl of Westerham's townhouse was, naturally, in the best part of town, away from the noise and pollution of the teeming city streets, but not so far from the park that Sebastian could not exercise his horse, or drive his high-perch phaeton.

He took himself to Whites to tell his acquaintances of his betrothal. It was imperative that the news of the engagement was spread before other gossip arrived in town. Someone was bound to hear about the riding debacle; such an exciting titbit of scandal would be greedily absorbed and hurried on its way.

By the end of the day Sebastian's face was stiff from smiling and his back sore from the congratulatory slapping. No one questioned his choice or his timing; he was the sole heir to a great name and it was his duty to produce sufficient sons to secure the title. What better way than choosing to marry his second cousin?

Too dispirited to join in any card

games or attend one of the soirées or musicals to which he had been invited, he returned home. He had done his duty, their reputations were safe. No wedding date had been set, but knowing the earl, it would be sooner rather than later. He scowled as he contemplated his future tied to a young woman with no sense of decorum and a figure like a boy's. She did have lovely eyes and a fine head of hair, but setting up his nursery with such a female did not fill him with enthusiasm.

The next morning he reported to his office at Horse Guards and discovered he was required to leave immediately for Belgium. Napoleon had escaped from Elba and was already in Paris, gathering loyal troops as fast as a dog found fleas. Wellington required his immediate services. He caught the next packet to Calais and was safely established on the Duke's staff within less than a week. All thoughts of Emily and their engagement were forgotten in the excitement of preparing for the inevitable battle with the French.

★   ★   ★

Meanwhile, at Westerham, Lady Althea slowly recovered both her looks and her spirits, even her straggly hair regained its lustre with the judicious use of henna. Emily rode out every day, sometimes with her sisters, sometimes accompanied only by a groom. She got to know her grandfather and finally forgave him for his neglect.

The ring, which had once been her grandmother's, remained unworn on her dresser. When the day came for their departure to London she had all but forgotten that she was engaged. Apart from the arrival of this token, with a brief note, they had received no communication from Viscount Yardley, which bothered her not one jot.

8

The Earl of Westerham asked Emily to visit him privately on the morning scheduled for their departure.

'Sit down, my dear; I am going to miss your company whilst you are in Town. Do not stop away too long.'

'We intend to return for the Yuletide festivities so it will be but five weeks we are absent.'

'Excellent; I have something special planned for you all. I am intending to hold a New Year's masquerade; Serena and Amelia will love it.'

'Will it not be too dark and dangerous for people to travel to Westerham, grandfather?'

He chuckled at her ignorance. 'Good heavens, my dear, my guests will already be here. I have invited fifty people to stay. The ball will be to celebrate your forthcoming nuptials.'

Emily shivered. 'I have noticed Emily, that you do not wear your betrothal ring. Is it a poor fit?'

She blushed. 'No, grandfather. It is remiss of me but I do not, as a rule, wear any jewellery. I am always afraid I will lose it. But I promise I shall put it on immediately.'

'Good girl; people will think it odd of you if you do not display it proudly. I believe Yardley will be returning soon; it is high time you spent some time together.'

'I am looking forward to it,' she lied. She stood up and came across to kiss her benefactor farewell. 'I am going to miss you, grandfather. You must take care of yourself whilst we are gone.'

He patted her cheek affectionately. 'I will, minx. And you enjoy yourself; attend as many parties and gatherings as you can, make some new friends. I have given Althea some extra cards so if there are any you wish to add to the house party, you will be free to do so.'

'Thank you; I must go, the carriage is

waiting. I must not keep the horses standing, it is cold this morning.'

★   ★   ★

The Gibson family made good time and arrived at Lessing House by mid-afternoon. There was still sufficient daylight for the girls to exclaim in delight at the place in which they were to reside for the next five weeks. Millie stood on the freshly washed pavement and stared up.

'There are four floors. It takes up quite half the block.' She gazed around the select square on which the house was situated. 'It is almost twice the size of all the other dwellings.'

'It is, my love. And it is as luxuriously appointed as Westerham. We will want for nothing, I promise you.'

'May I play in a little garden in the centre, Mama? It has a lawn and flowerbeds and there are statues of ladies in it,' Serena asked.

'I am sure Mary will take you when

the weather is fine, if Miss Quenby gives you leave.'

The governess, a sprightly, middle-aged lady of superior knowledge and impeccable references, nodded and smiled. 'Your mornings will still be spent on your books, Miss Serena, but I think the afternoons can be given over to visits and excursions. After all this is your first time in our capital city. I am sure Lady Althea wishes you to see as much of it is possible.'

'Indeed I do, Miss Quenby. Miss Gibson and I will be out a deal of the time so I am trusting you to plan a suitable itinerary for my youngest daughters.'

'Miss Quenby has promised she will take us to the Tower and the Vauxhall Gardens. I am so pleased to be here, Mama, I think I might burst.'

'I do hope not, Miss Serena, it would make such a mess on this clean pavement,' Miss Quenby replied smiling.

The London butler, Digby, from his

vantage point at the head of the steps, viewed the laughing group with disfavour.

Emily noticed the front door was open and bright candlelight spilling out. 'Come along, everyone, I think we should go in.' She noticed the look on the butler's face and realized they had been making a spectacle of themselves, gawping like villagers at a fair.

Digby showed them in and introduced the rest of the staff to Lady Althea. Then they were conducted to their apartments at the far side of the spacious building. In every room welcoming fires burnt merrily and candelabrum glowed with expensive beeswax candles. The youngest girls had been put, with Miss Quenby and Mary, on the attic floor in the nursery wing. They were not impressed.

'Why do we have to be up here? It's cold and dark. Grandfather does not make us sleep in the nurseries,' Serena said crossly.

'Indeed he does not, my loves. Nor

shall you this visit.' Lady Althea turned to the housekeeper. 'Miss Amelia and Miss Serena will have rooms next to Miss Gibson. And you will find a more comfortable chamber for Miss Quenby.'

'Yes, my lady. I'm sorry, my lady, but Mr Digby believes that children belong in the nursery, not on the second floor.'

Lady Althea smiled. 'I quite understand. Mary you can remain up here, Jenny and Edwards can join you. When you have fires burning it will be quite cosy.'

The girls' belongings were packed and transported back downstairs. It was full dark by the time the party was settled to everyone's satisfaction. After a light supper, served in a pretty withdrawing-room on the first floor, the girls were so tired they went to bed without demure, leaving Emily and her mother alone.

'I think I am going to retire also, my dear, I am fatigued after the journey.' Emily rang the bell and a parlour maid appeared to escort her mother to her rooms.

'I am going to explore for a while. I want to discover the whereabouts of the library and the study. Miss Quenby wishes to use one of them for her lessons.' Emily waited for the young maid to return to guide her downstairs. 'Are the rooms on the ground floor not open, Beth?' she asked the girl on the way down the richly carpeted stairs.

'They are, Miss Gibson; but they're for Viscount Yardley's use.' The girl grinned. 'Your coming has fair put old Digby out of sorts, I can tell you, miss. He cannot abide either women or children. I am up from Westerham, same as you; all female staff are, including Mrs Lawford. She is under housekeeper back there.' The girl halted in front of a stout door. 'This is the library, Miss Gibson. Shall I show you the study too?'

'Yes, please do. Why are there are no flowers anywhere?'

Beth giggled. 'Old sour face can't

abide flowers neither. Shall I send out for some tomorrow, Miss Gibson?'

'Yes, Lady Althea likes the house to be filled with blooms. Will someone go to Covent Garden for them?'

'That they will, Miss Gibson. If Mrs Lawford allows, I'll go myself, and take a couple of boot boys along with me to carry them.'

Emily decided that the study, although presently unlit and chilly, would be more than adequate for her sisters to take their lessons.

'I can find my way back to my rooms, thank you, Beth, so you can go. I intend to sit in the library for a while and read. I noticed it has a decent fire burning.'

'Very well, Miss Gibson. If you're sure. Goodnight, miss.'

Beth vanished through a door in the panelling, leaving Emily alone outside the library. Feeling a little like an intruder she pushed open the door and went in. The rows of leather bound books were mostly dull and of no interest but she found a volume on the history of London and took that back to a comfortable, deep-seated, leather chair, positioned close to the fire.

She tucked her feet under her, smoothing out the delicate folds of the skirt of her green spotted muslin. She was glad this gown had long sleeves and that she had thought to place a cashmere shawl around her shoulders. The candles she had positioned on the mantelshelf and small side tables bathed her in a golden glow. The combination of warmth and exhaustion caused her head to droop and she fell asleep.

She did not hear the sound of the carriage outside or the bustle as another visitor arrived. She slept through. The candles burned down lower and the fire went out. The cold finally woke her. The feeble glow of the two remaining candle stubs revealed little. Then she felt the heavy weight in her lap and remembered where she was.

She uncurled her legs with difficulty and stumbled to her feet. Her dress was creased and her hair, as usual, was falling down around her face. Crossly she pulled out the remaining pins and shook her head, sending the waist length curls cascading down her back in a russet waterfall.

The large clock, ticking loudly in its wooden case, told her it was past midnight. Everyone would be asleep. She frowned; why had Jenny not sought her out? Had the girls not missed their usual goodnight embrace?

One of the candles guttered and went out. Quickly Emily snatched up the remaining one; she had to find a room with fresh candles before she was left in the pitch black to grope her way back to her rooms.

The feeble glimmer showed her the door and she opened it quietly, not wishing to wake the household. She stood, holding her candle aloft, staring down the long dark passageway. Then to her delight she saw a crack of yellow escaping from a door further down. It was in the opposite direction to the one she knew she must take but, if there was someone in the room, they could provide her with directions and the necessary illumination.

She did not stop to consider exactly who that someone might be. It was only as she tentatively pushed the door open that it occurred to her the room could be occupied by an intruder. In her terror she dropped the candle and plunged herself into total darkness. She had to flee, but disorientated by the lack of light, she had no idea in which direction to go. Too late she heard the sound of rapidly approaching footsteps and the door crashed open.

Emily tried to press herself against the wall and she prayed for deliverance; what she got was a lethal blow to her right temple and she collapsed, without a sound, at her attacker's feet.

★   ★   ★

'God's teeth!' Sebastian swore and dropped to his knees in horror. He had known the minute his clenched fist landed that he had made a terrible mistake. It was only now that he appreciated just how bad. He had thought he had felled a house-maid on an illicit night time jaunt, but this was so much worse.

In the light from his sitting-room he gently scooped his unconscious fiancé up and her unbound hair spilled over his arms in warm thick ripples. Its soft touch made his stomach clench and his pulse accelerate.

Carefully he laid Emily on the nearest sofa. He dropped again to his knees and pushed back the hair from her face. He swore again, more viciously. The vivid purple bruise already appearing on her temple was ample evidence of his brute force. He looked around for something to press on the swelling. There were only the dregs of his claret decanter. It would have to do. He tipped the thick ruby liquid onto the neck-cloth he had removed earlier.

The red stains left by the damp cloth matched the spreading bruise. Should he call for assistance? How was he to explain the presence of his fiancé, with hair unbound, unconscious in his private quarters? Whatever explanation was offered it would be disbelieved. The evidence spoke for itself. It had been an assignation in which they had violently disagreed and, in his fury, he had struck her down.

A faint sound alerted him. She was coming to her senses. He saw her eyelids flicker and open. He stared into her extraordinary hazel eyes and his chest constricted. How could he ever have thought her plain? She was the most beautiful and desirable woman he had ever seen.

★   ★   ★

Slowly, Emily returned to full consciousness. Her head hurt and her vision was blurred. Then she remembered the door opening and the violent blow to her head. She stiffened and fear flooded back. She was trapped, helpless, with the monster who had tried to kill her. She felt herself falling back into a black pit. From a distance she heard a familiar voice.

'Emily, it is I, Sebastian. You are safe; I will not hurt you again. It was an accident. I thought you were an intruder.'

She lay still, assimilating his words, trying to make sense from them. It was Sebastian who had treated her so cruelly? But he was in Belgium, how could he be here in London? She felt a soothing coolness on her throbbing temple and, although she did not fully understand what she heard, she knew they were words of comfort. She sighed, relaxed and slipped into a deep restorative slumber.

★ ★ ★

Sebastian bent down and rested his fingers under her jaw, seeking for her pulse. It was strong and regular. He thanked God she was asleep and not unconscious again. Sebastian watched her, glad his blow had apparently not caused her serious harm.

He uncoiled, rubbing his unshaven jaw, his expression troubled. He was, for the first time in his adult life, at a loss to know how to proceed. He could not carry her, undetected, upstairs to her rooms, because he did not know exactly where she had been placed. But neither could he leave her here, in his chambers, she would be hopelessly compromised. Even engaged couples could not indulge in such wanton behaviour.

What he needed were servants who were discreet and totally loyal. His man, Smith, was one; and he was certain Emily's abigail would be another. He pulled the bell and waited impatiently.

'Smith, I have a problem. If Miss Gibson and I are to come out of this unscathed I am going to need your help.'

Smith, an intelligent man, took in the

situation at a glance. He had the sense not to ask questions. If he had seen the bruise marring Emily's face he might not have been so helpful but it was conveniently covered by her hair.

'I need to know which chamber Miss Gibson has been given. I also need her maid down here immediately.'

'Yes, sir.' Smith vanished leaving Sebastian to pace anxiously. Ten minutes later his servant reappeared, Jenny at his side.

'I have been beside myself with worry, my lord, when Miss Emily did not return. I didn't know what do for the best.' Jenny hurried over to her mistress puzzled that she lay so still. She was more observant than Smith. 'What has happened here, my lord? Has there been an accident?' She knelt beside Emily who stirred a little but did not wake.

Viscount Yardley coughed and cleared his throat, unwilling to admit that it was he who had caused the injury. 'I startled Miss Gibson and she fell, hitting her head; but you will find that she is asleep, not unconscious.'

Jenny sniffed, which did not endear her to his lordship. 'She should be in her own bed, sir, not down here on your settle.'

He ground his teeth. 'If you would take me to her rooms, she will be in her bed soon enough.' Sebastian, Emily cradled in his arms, followed Jenny, with her candle high, along the black, silent corridors. Smith padded along in front quietly opening and closing the doors.

The warm weight of his sleeping fiancé felt right in Sebastian's arms. Her head nestled trustingly on his shoulder and she had slid her arm around his neck when he lifted her.

On reaching her bedchamber he released her reluctantly, putting her carefully on her bed. He stepped back, barely resisting the temptation to drop a kiss on her brow. Smith lit his passage back, allowing him to follow, immersed in his thoughts.

He realized he was more than reconciled to his forthcoming marriage. Life with Emily would never be dull. He smiled widely. From this point forward he was determined to turn his considerable charm and diplomatic skill to winning his young fiancé's heart.

* * *

Emily opened her eyes and attempted to lift her head but an agonizing pain shot from her temple to her jaw, forcing her to lie still. The shutters were still drawn and she could see sunlight through the cracks. It was morning; it was time to summon her abigail. She tried a second time to rise and her world spun and the intensity of the pain sickened her. She closed her eyes until the unpleasant swirling sensations had ceased.

Jenny had heard her struggles and came bursting in. 'Now, you stay put, Miss Emily. You took a nasty tumble last night and banged your head. I have informed Lady Althea and she's on her way to see you.'

Emily felt too unwell to argue. She raised a feeble hand to indicate her agreement but made no attempt to speak. Her brain would not engage itself and it was too much effort to marshal her tangled thoughts.

Lady Althea arrived and was horrified to find her older daughter prostrate. 'My darling girl, this is too bad. I am sending for the doctor right away. It is a great pity as I planned to introduce you to society today. We have cards for an elegant musical soirée at Lady Armitage's house; it would have been the perfect venue for you to make your curtsy.'

Emily forced her tongue, which felt, and acted, like a piece of wet lamb's wool, to form an answer. 'You go to the soirée without me, Mama. It would be a shame for both of us to miss it.'

'Very well, my dear; if the doctor pronounces you well enough for me to leave you.' She glanced around the room searching for clues. 'Jenny, what exactly did Miss Gibson trip over?'

Jenny coloured. 'I've no idea, my lady. I was elsewhere when it happened. I helped Miss Emily into her bed, that's all.'

'It is all very odd.' Lady Althea smiled. 'But no doubt when Miss Gibson has recovered she will be able to tell us exactly what transpired.'

Jenny curtsied and retired to the safety of the dressing room. She rather doubted that the full truth of the matter would ever be revealed, and especially not to Lady Althea.

9

The doctor pronounced Emily to be suffering from a mild concussion and confined her to her bed until he visited again. She felt so wretched that she did not argue. She slept most of the day. She was unaware that twice Smith had arrived with messages from his master. At teatime Emily had recovered sufficiently to drink a little barley water, but still felt too nauseous to eat.

'Your sisters have called, twice, but the doctor said that you were to have no visitors today, apart from Lady Althea,' Jenny told her mistress. She did not mention the missives from Viscount Yardley that remained unopened on the side table. In her opinion that gentleman was more culpable then he owned.

At dusk Emily finally felt well enough to sit up. She had an urgent need to find the commode. She rang the small brass bell her maid had placed by her bed and waited, uncomfortably, for assistance.

Her head spun unpleasantly and she was glad to regain her bed. She noticed the unopened letters on the table and asked Jenny to hand them to her. She unfolded one and the strong black writing leapt from the paper.

My dear Emily,

I am devastated to find you so unwell. Last night I had no idea you had sustained a concussion. I cannot begin to tell you how sorry I am. Can you ever forgive me?

Yours affectionately,
Yardley.

Frowning Emily opened the second letter. This should have been read before the other.

Dear Emily,

Please could you come to the rose

garden at eleven o'clock, I wish to speak with you in private.

Yours respectfully,
Yardley

Incensed she felt her head throb as the blood pulsed in waves around her body. It mattered not that the horrid brute had mistaken her for a burglar; that was no excuse, for no robber would be wearing a dress or have hair down to their waist.

She twisted the emerald ring around her finger, tempted to tear it off and return it. Then sanity prevailed. No, she would allow the engagement to continue for the present, but the minute she was established in society the engagement ended. For however much her grandfather wished it, she was never going to tie herself of a man so steeped in drink and violence that he could mistake a woman for a burglar.

★ ★ ★

'Where is it we are going this evening, Mama?'

'The Galvestons are throwing a ball to celebrate their eldest daughter's engagement to Lord Brackley. Although it is not a fashionable time to hold such an event I am sure it will be a sad crush. The Galvestons are famous for their parties. Are you certain you are up to it, my dear?'

Emily nodded and felt no ill effects. 'I'm fully recovered, thank you. It's high time I wore one of my grand evening gowns.'

'Viscount Yardley is in residence, Emily, my love. I know you have not been well enough to see him but it would have been advantageous for him to escort us on your first appearance. After all, he is supposed to be your betrothed. Unfortunately he told me he does not have an invitation.'

'I am relieved to hear it, Mama, as I have no desire to spend an evening in his company.'

'The card states nine o'clock, but as

it could take an hour for the carriage to deliver us we will leave at eight o'clock.' She glanced at the mantle clock. 'I have ordered a light repast to be served to us in our rooms at six. This will leave us ample time to complete our preparations.'

Emily could not imagine how changing one's dress could possibly take so long. 'I have not seen the girls today; I believe I heard them returning from their excursion a moment ago. I am going to find out how they enjoyed their visit to the Tower. The lions are always a splendid sight.'

Her supper was waiting for her when she returned to her own room. Although she was no longer suffering from a headache her appetite had not returned. She viewed the cold cuts, bread-and-butter and pickles with disfavour.

Jenny appeared from the bedchamber. 'Oh miss, I was becoming anxious. Your bath has been waiting this past half-hour.'

'I am coming immediately. I still have an hour before I need to be downstairs.'

She soon discovered why her mother had suggested allowing two hours for her toilette. Her elaborate hair style took so long she had barely ten minutes to put on her first real evening gown. Lady Althea had wanted her to have all three made up in pastel shades and white for these were the expected colours for a debutante. Emily had refused. This, as far as she could see, was the only advantage that being betrothed to Viscount Yardley presented. An engaged young lady was allowed more flexibility in her choice of colour.

She had selected emerald green silk for the under skirt and a filmy silver gauze for the over dress. The bodice, cut low as fashion demanded, curved prettily over her bosom. Her mother had lent her necklace of square cut emeralds, set in silver, which complemented her outfit perfectly.

'There, miss, you're ready. I haven't

pulled you in too tight, there's no need, you're still so slender.' Jenny stepped back to admire her mistress. 'You look a picture, Miss Emily. And no one could possibly mistake you for a boy tonight.'

Emily glanced down and grinned. 'I do appear to have blossomed in that area, do I not?' She ran the silk through her fingers. 'I feel like a fairytale princess. It's a pity I don't have a Prince Charming to accompany me.'

Jenny handed Emily the ribbon attached to her demi-train, her matching reticule, and fan. 'I hope I don't trip myself up, Jenny. I can't imagine how I shall manage to dance with so many bits and pieces to hold.'

'You give your reticule and fan to Lady Althea whilst you dance, miss.'

'I'm delighted to hear it. I wish you were coming too; it seems unfair only one abigail is allowed to accompany us.'

A tap on the door reminded Emily she was late. Jenny opened the door and a footman announced that the carriage was waiting outside. In a swirl of green silk Emily followed him along passageways and downstairs. Halfway down she risked a glance over the banisters. She stopped dead.

'Mama, you look *ravisante*! I hardly recognized you in that fabulous gown.'

Lady Althea smiled up at her daughter, poised like a green angel, on the stairs. 'And so do you, my love. What a spectacular pair we shall be. You will be surrounded by eligible young men, just you wait and see.'

Emily continued her descent and her gurgling laughter echoed round the entrance hall. 'I hope not, Mama. I do not wish Sebastian to feel obliged to call anyone out.' Her humorous reply was sufficient reminder of her status.

'I really meant you will not lack for partners, my love. Even an engaged lady is permitted to dance with suitable young gentlemen. But no more than once, but I am sure you already understand that rule.'

'I do indeed. I'm only permitted to

stand up more than once with my fiancé.'

A footman handed them into the carriage. Its candle lamps bobbed and dipped in the darkness, the two horses stamped, their breath swirling in clouds around their handsome heads. Edwards checked that Emily's silver-lined evening cloak was safely inside the coach and that Lady Althea's ruby-red creation was resting smoothly on the seat, then they were ready to leave.

'This is the first time I have been out in a city in the dark, Mama. It's a thrilling experience.' Emily peered out of the window, catching glimpses of street vendors and late shoppers on the overcrowded pavements. As expected it was an hour before the carriage finally pulled up at the steps of Galveston House. Blazing flambeaux illuminated the illustrious company attempting to gain access. The steps were already full of ladies of various ages dressed in their finest, and gentleman in black tailcoats and knee-breeches or pantaloons.

Emily stared at the jostling people

on the steps with horror. She hated crowds. 'I think I shall go home again, Mama. I have a headache.'

Lady Althea stared hard at her daughter. 'You shall do no such thing, Emily. We are here now, and whether you like it or not, in we will go.'

Emily's shoulders drooped and her mother's expression softened. 'You do not have to remain long if you are truly unwell, my love. Edwards will be waiting in a withdrawing-room and she can summon the carriage to return whenever you wish.'

A liveried footman, his gold frogging glittering in the torchlight, assisted them from the carriage. Edwards shook out their skirts and they shuffled forward with the rest. Once inside Emily began to enjoy herself. There was so much to see. There were older guests still wearing elaborate wigs and white face paint with black beauty spots. Some gentlemen were still dressed in the earlier fashion of brightly coloured evening coats, bedecked with silver and huge gold buttons.

Girls of similar age to her were, she noticed, uniformly dressed in white or pastel shades. For an instant she wished she had paid heed to her mother, but then she held up her head and her beautiful hazel eyes flashed defiantly. She was not an insipid debutante on the lookout for a rich husband; she had a ring already on her finger.

At last Emily and her mother were making their curtsey. Lady Galveston greeted them with unrestrained delight. Much kissing of cheeks and exclaiming took place before they were sent on their way to join the milling crowd thronging the Grand Salon. Lady Althea sailed ahead, the ostrich feathers in her head waving gaily.

'We shall sit here, my love, close to the dance floor.' A lovely blonde girl sitting demurely on a chair next to her own mama smiled a welcome.

Emily smiled back. 'I am Emily Gibson; this is my very first ball.' Her neighbour glanced to her mother for permission before answering.

'I am Maria Fitzwilliam. I came out this summer, and this is only the third ball I have attended.'

Lady Althea nodded to Mrs Fitzwilliam and she nodded back. Contact established, the older women settled down for a comfortable coze. The Fitzwilliams were an excellent family and extremely well-connected. Edwards disappeared, discreetly, with their cloaks and Emily's spare slippers.

A footman approached with a tray of champagne, followed closely by one with a tray of orgeat. The trays appeared identical. With a grin at her new friend Emily daringly selected champagne, Maria sensibly took the non-alcoholic beverage.

Maria spotted Emily's engagement ring. Long gloves were *de rigueur* but it was permissible to have them finishing at the knuckles if one so wished.

'Miss Gibson, you are betrothed. How lucky you are. I have still to find anyone remotely suitable.'

Lady Althea smiled at her disingenuous remark. 'Viscount Yardley is an excellent match. My father, the Earl of Westerham, is delighted that his heir is to marry his granddaughter.'

Maria was suitably impressed and Mrs Fitzwilliam as delighted as their hostess that such a lovely young heiress was already off the marriage mart.

'Are you expecting Viscount Yardley to attend tonight?' Maria inquired politely.

'No; I believe he is otherwise engaged. He is a diplomat and his time is not his own,' Lady Althea answered.

Emily sipped her drink, enjoying the way the bubbles tickled her nose. It tasted delicious, cold and crisp. She took a large swallow and to her astonishment her world appeared to tilt alarmingly. Could it be her injury or this innocuous looking drink?

An ungloved, male hand, reached over and removed the glass from her grasp. 'I believe, my love, that you have mistakenly selected champagne.'

Her eyes flew up to meet the amused gaze of her fiancé. She was about to protest when a warning in his eyes made her swallow the words. She smiled ruefully as he pulled her to her feet.

'I did not expect to see you here tonight, Sebastian, but I am pleased, of course, that you have come.'

All four women were now on their feet. He bowed deeply to Lady Althea. 'I am delighted to see you looking so well, Lady Althea. It is quite clear from whom your daughter has inherited her beauty.'

Lady Althea simpered and quite forgot she did not like her great-nephew. 'Allow me to introduce Mrs Fitzwilliam and her daughter, Miss Fitzwilliam, to you, my lord.'

He bowed to Mrs Fitzwilliam and nodded and smiled at Maria. 'I believe the first set is forming, shall we go, my dear?'

Emily was given no choice in the matter, but was whisked away down the ballroom to join the other couples. She was not usually lost for words, but this handsome man, resplendent in full evening rig, his blonde hair shining, his cravat falling in snowy folds, held in place by a single emerald pin, was like a stranger. A very attractive stranger.

She had seen him in his riding gear and in his country evening apparel but dressed as he was, in black, he looked magnificent. Every debutante's dream, a real-life Prince Charming. Then she recalled that scarcely three days before he had knocked her unconscious and she still had the bruise to prove it.

She attempted to snatch her arm from his but his grip tightened. He bent his mouth to whisper in her ear, to onlookers it appeared merely the gesture of a man besotted, but they could not hear his words.

'You will not cause a scene here, Emily. You are a child no longer, it would do you good to remember that.'

She tried a second time, more subtly, to remove her hand. 'I will not stand up with you and neither will I marry you. You're an unspeakable brute,' she hissed.

'If you persist in this nonsense you will see just how much of a brute I can be, my girl. Now, behave yourself. This is not the time for such discussions.'

'Then when? I promise you, I will not dance until I have an answer I am satisfied with.'

'We will talk later on the terrace, after this dance is finished.' Her resistance ceased and with a false smiled pinned to her face she allowed him to guide her to the set. She dipped and curtsied, skipped and galloped when required, outwardly a beautiful young woman enjoying her debut in the company of her fiancé.

Lady Althea watched with a proud smile. She was basking in her daughter's success. Several old acquaintances had drifted over to see her and complimented her on her own appearance. Happy that her daughter was in good hands she accepted an invitation to play a hand of whist in one of the side rooms set aside for that purpose.

Emily allowed her fiancé to lead her from the floor and she was dismayed to find her mother no longer in her appointed place. She was regretting her rash challenge and wished heartily to back out of the promised *tête à tête*. The uncompromising set of Viscount Yardley's shoulders and the grimness of his features did not bode well.

'My mother is not here, sir. I do not have her permission to go out on the terrace.'

'You need no permission; you are under my protection.' He threaded her smartly through the press of people and outside. There were several other couples already there, cooling down after their exertions on the dance floor.

'It's too cold here, I wish to go in again, if you please. I do not want to catch a chill.'

Without a word he swung around and marched her back inside. She could feel the muscles of his forearm tighten. Where was he taking her? Where was her mother? She wriggled her fingers but they were held firm. Then from feeling fearful she was flooded with righteous indignation.

How dare this man drag her, against her will, about the place? Ignoring the two couples standing quietly talking, she flung her weight backwards, taking her captor by surprise. His grip slackened and she was free. Every instinct told her to make good her escape but her anger made her brave.

She stood her ground and stared at Sebastian, icy rage in her eyes. 'Enough, sir. I will not be manhandled like this. I will speak with you here, and you will listen.' That four other people were riveted also did not bother her. She removed her ring and held it out. 'Here, sir, this I believe, is yours. I want none of it.'

* * *

Too astonished to protest he instinctively held out his hand and felt his token drop into his palm. He stared at it in disbelief. By the time he had recovered his ex-fiancé had vanished into the ballroom. How could this have happened? She had made him a laughing stock. Word of his dismissal would already be passing round the gathering like wildfire.

His fists closed and the jewel bit into his palm. He took several deep breaths. His fury burned inside him, but he banked it down. Apparently unconcerned he smiled at the interested spectators, casually slipped the ring into his waistcoat pocket, and sauntered off, as though he had not a care in the world.

No one would have suspected that before the night was out he intended to deal out a punishment to Emily that would necessitate her taking all her meals standing up for the foreseeable future.

In the ballroom Emily was instantly engulfed in a sea of gentlemen all eager to scribble their names on her dance card. She had no intention of honouring these assignations. She wanted to return home, at once, but until she found her mother, she was trapped. Any moment she feared that the man she had just publicly jilted would appear to exact his revenge.

10

Emily nodded, dipped and smiled, promising she was to return in a few moments, but always moving steadily away from the double doors that led to the passageway. She hoped she could hide herself in the crowd, but suspected that her vivid green gown and chestnut hair would make her easy to spot.

She found herself in the almost empty receiving hall, all the expected guests having arrived. Lord and Lady Galveston and their daughter Sophia and her fiancé had deserted their post on the stairs that led down to the lower floors and freedom.

Emily hesitated, should she go up or down? Edwards was upstairs waiting; downstairs somewhere she would find the carriage. She made her decision and ran upstairs, her dress held high, exposing far more ankle than was seemly.

A helpful chambermaid appeared at her side and guided her to the rooms in which the ladies could retire and repair the ravages of an evening on the dance floor. On enquiring Emily discovered that all the maids, dressers, and abigails were elsewhere but the girl promised Edwards would be fetched to her immediately.

She felt as if her heart was trying to escape the confines of her bodice; her mouth was dry and intermittent tremors shook her tall, slender frame. The other ladies in the room watched her covertly; like colourful vultures they waited, certain they would be able to pick up some juicy gossip to tell their friends.

The servant's door opened and Edwards hurried in. She had Emily's green and silver cloak over her arm.

'I am sorry you are feeling unwell, Miss Emily. I have asked for the carriage to be brought round at once.'

Emily quickly took her cue. 'I think I was imprudent to come out so soon after my fall, Edwards. I should have heeded the doctor's advice and rested a few days longer.' Edwards cleverly brushed Emily's hair aside revealing the livid purple blue bruise that marred the right side of her forehead and ran back into her curls.

The watchers sighed — no gossip here — the flushed girl was merely unwell. With an injury like that on her temple, it was hardly surprising.

'I should sit down, Miss Emily. It might be some time before they send for us. The carriage could be several streets away.'

Emily allowed herself to be seated on a *chaise-longue*. 'What about Lady Althea? How will she return if I take the carriage?'

'Do not fret, miss; I have sent a message to Lady Althea; she's quite content to wait until it returns to collect her. She's in no hurry to leave.'

Ladies came and went but still they did not receive the longed for summons. Emily flinched every time the door opened expecting a furious Viscount Yardley to burst in and accost her. It was a full forty-five minutes before a footman arrived to escort them. The sound of the quartet playing and the tinkle of laughter accompanied Emily for it was almost midnight and the ball was in full swing.

Emily saw no one she knew as she hurried down with Edwards close behind her. At the door she turned.

'I can return alone, Edwards. I wish you to remain here in case Lady Althea needs you.'

Edwards did not protest. 'Very well, miss. I will see you to the carriage and then return to wait.'

Emily mounted the carriage steps and felt her fear slip away; she sank back onto the silken squabs in the welcome darkness of the spacious interior. Edwards stepped back and the steps were folded. The door closed, the coachman clicked and the horses shook their heads.

With a sigh of relief she settled

herself more comfortably. She was safe, at least until the morning, and by that time, she prayed, Sebastian would have calmed down. Something, a slight noise, an almost imperceptible movement at the far side of the coach, alerted her. She did not turn her head, she did not need to. She was not alone. The man she was so desperate to escape from was inside the carriage with her.

Icy tremors ran down her spine. She was trapped. He was a violent man — had he not already mowed her down? And servants, if they valued their positions, did not interfere in their master's business.

She must not give herself away. He must not know she was aware of him. Her hand slid across to the door handle and began to lift it. She kept her face averted, pretending she was sleeping, praying he would not announce his presence for a few seconds longer.

There, she felt it move. Without conscious thought, so terrified she did not stop to consider the consequences, Emily threw open the door and jumped out into the darkness, glad the horses were still at a walk. She thought she heard him shout but, remembering her frequent falls when learning to ride her pony years ago, curled herself into a ball to land on the cobbles, shoulder first.

The impact jarred the breath from her body but, otherwise unhurt, she scrambled to her feet and gathering her cloak about her she fled down the pavement, heedless of her surroundings, only wishing to escape from the man in the coach. Even the short time she had been inside with him, she had been aware of the anger pulsing towards her. She knew he hated her, knew he intended to do her harm.

She heard him call after her but this only made her run faster. She ran round corner after corner until she was sure she was safe from her pursuer. She collapsed against a railing, gulping in air, hoping to discover where her mad dash had taken her. The light from the full moon showed that she was in a residential road away from the main thoroughfare. Tall houses loomed on either side, their windows dark and uninviting. What had she been thinking of? No girl of sense would leap from the safety of a carriage and take to the streets unprotected.

She felt her fear flood back; it would have been better to have faced Sebastian, but it was too late to repine. If she could retrace her path and return to the main route at least there she might recognize her whereabouts.

Her slippers were ruined, her dress and cloak torn, her elaborate hairstyle in disarray. Then she remembered her jewels. Her fingers flew to her head; the tiara was still in place. She pulled it out and then carefully removed her long ear bobs and unfastened her necklace; there was no point in advertising her wealth.

She opened her reticule, luckily still suspended from her wrist, and was about to drop them in when she reconsidered. Perhaps her jewellery would be safer concealed somewhere on her person. She dropped the precious items into the bag then hastily lifted her skirts and tied the ribbon to her drawers. She smoothed down her skirt and could see no telltale bulge. Satisfied she had done all she could to protect her mother's heirlooms she began to walk back, hoping her stupidity would not end in disaster.

Even Sebastian's anger began to seem preferable to being alone, cold and footsore, at midnight in a deserted London street. Her heart skipped as, in the distance, she heard the welcome sound of carriage wheels on cobbles. She increased her pace, the sooner she was back on the main thoroughfare the better.

She emerged, bedraggled and weary, to see the tail-lights of a carriage bobbing away in the distance. The wide street was otherwise abandoned. No linkmen, no gentlemen returning foxed from their clubs. She had no idea where she was or what direction to turn in. It started to rain. Miserably she trudged on. She rounded the corner and on seeing a group of young bucks walking down the opposite pavement shrunk into the shadows, hoping they would pass by unaware.

'What ho? I spy a fair damsel,' one of them called, and leaving his companions to follow if they wished, he lurched from the path and headed towards Emily.

She had no option, face them or flee. She stepped away from the wall and back straight, expression severe, she waited, every inch a lady, however unlikely that might appear. The inebriated young man stopped. He bowed, almost pitching onto his face in the gutter. He smiled, but it did not reach his eyes.

'Can I be of assistance, my fair lady? You appear to be in some distress.'

Emily tried to think of a plausible explanation. She could hear the rattle of a carriage approaching at speed. Then the crash of a door and running footsteps and she was swept from her feet into a crushing embrace.

'You little idiot! What were you thinking of?' Sebastian turned to her would be rescuer. 'I thank you, sir, for your kind offer, but my fiancée is safe with me.'

The first of the man's two companions had, by this time, joined him and, even as drunk as they were, they realized that their prey was lost to them. This tall, formidable gentleman had murder in his eyes. They backed away, bowing and muttering pleasantries, leaving Emily and Sebastian alone on the path.

Uncontrollable shivers racked her body and her knees began to buckle. 'Come, sweetheart, I will take you home. We can talk in the morning when we are both recovered.'

Emily snuggled into Sebastian's warm arms and felt safe and cosseted. From fearsome ogre he had been transformed, in her muddled mind, to gallant saviour. On arrival at Lessing House, he carried her swiftly through the deserted corridors and left her in the capable hands of her maid, who was beginning to wonder why her young lady always returned injured and in disarray, when in the Viscount's company.

* * *

Emily did not stir until noon the next day. She suffered no ill effects from her exploits but her beautiful evening dress and cloak were ruined beyond repair. She had a leisurely bath and selected an especially becoming sprigged muslin morning-gown in pale peach. Her head was aching a trifle so she asked Jenny to braid her hair loosely and leave it in a single, shiny plait hanging down her back.

The enormity of her behaviour, from the public humiliation of her fiancé to the stupid leap out of the carriage, filled her with remorse and shame. She knew she had to face the reckoning some-time, so it might as well be now.

'Jenny, do you know if Viscount Yardley is in the house?'

'Yes, miss, he sent a message enquiring after your health and said he would be waiting for you in the library, whatever time you rose.' Emily shuddered. 'Are you unwell, miss? I hope you have not caught a chill from your experiences last night.'

'I am sure I have not, thank you. I am very fortunate to feel no effects, apart from a stiff shoulder.'

Her maid offered no comment. How anybody could manage to fall from a moving carriage she could not imagine, unless that Viscount had been up to his tricks again. And why had Miss Emily's reticule been fastened to her drawers? It was a mystery, and no mistake.

'Do you wish me to accompany you downstairs, miss? I could sit quietly and act as chaperone.'

'It's a kind offer, but no, I think not.' Emily almost smiled, as she imagined

Sebastian's expression if she arrived with her maid in tow.

She paused outside the library to steady her racing pulse and tidy her skirts. Her head was throbbing and her shoulder ached abominably. She smiled ruefully, it was no more than she deserved. She wanted to turn and run back upstairs to the sanctuary of her bedchamber, but that would only postpone this unpleasant interview.

Gathering her failing courage she pushed open the door and stepped in, unconsciously bracing herself for an onslaught of abuse. Sebastian had been staring out of the window at the rain dripping from the trees. He heard the door and swung round, his expression severe. But when he saw the beautiful, ashen faced girl, framed in the doorway, his face changed instantly to concern.

He strode across to take her limp, cold hands in his, chafing them to bring back some warmth.

'Emily, you pea-goose, you should not be up. You do not look at all the thing.' He led her, unresisting, to a well padded settle, pulled up close to the fire. 'Sit here, sweetheart. I have already rung for some hot chocolate. Maybe that will restore some colour to your cheeks.'

This unexpected kindness was Emily's undoing. Her eyes filled and tears trickled unchecked down her face.

'God's teeth! I am a brute,' she heard him swear, not for the first time. Then she was on his lap, with his arms firmly around her. 'I do not mean to frighten you, darling, you must know that I would never harm a single hair on your head.'

Emily raised her tearstained face to his, a watery smile curving her lips. 'Unless I drive you to it by my irresponsible and unforgivable behaviour.'

He chuckled, wiping away her tears with his thumbs. 'I admit last night my intention was to spank some sense into your lovely head.'

She settled more comfortably into his arms. 'And now?'

'And now, I find to my astonishment that I have forgiven you, again.' He frowned, his *volte-face* sending shock waves down her spine. Her fear reflected on her face. 'Do not panic, you silly girl; I shall not do it this time. But, I promise, if ever you do anything so stupid again you will sincerely regret it.'

Emily raised her eyebrows. 'I can assure you, I have no intention of jilting you in public a second time.'

He shook his head in disbelief. 'I do not give a damn for that. I am talking about jumping from a moving carriage and running away into the night. I have never been so scared. Even Boney's crack troops have not engendered such fear in me. I thought I would not find you in time.' He bent his head and touched his lips to hers in a gentle kiss.

'I find,' he said, when he finally raised his head, 'that you have stolen my heart, little cousin. I did not know such a thing could happen, and so fast.'

Her smile was radiant. 'And I,

although I have fought hard not to, have become besotted with you, Cousin Sebastian.'

'What ever are we going to do about it?'

'I cannot imagine, I am quite at a loss.'

In answer he pulled her tightly to his heart. 'Can you feel it, darling? It beats just for you. How soon can I persuade you to marry me?' He smoothed her hair, and touched his lips softly to her bruised face. 'I can not imagine why you love me, Emily. I have behaved appallingly. I am, I promise you, known throughout Europe as a calm and reasonable man, not given to wild tempers and uncontrollable rages.'

She laughed and, wriggling free of his loose grip, resumed her seat on the sofa. 'And I do not, as a rule, behave like a hoyden with as much common-sense as a chicken.' Her ringless hand still rested in his.

'I have something to ask you, my love. Will you marry me? Will you do me the honour of becoming my wife?

Will you make me the happiest man in England? You must answer me from your heart. I will understand if you feel that you cannot tie yourself to a brute like me.'

Her answering smile made his heart turn over. 'I love you, and you love me, that is all I ever wanted in a match. I do not care how volatile our relationship will prove to be; if we truly love each other, it will survive.'

Instantly he looked younger, more like the man of scarcely four and twenty that he was. He smiled and his eyes bored into hers. 'You still have not answered my question. Are you going to marry me? And how soon?'

She tipped her head as she considered. 'Well, I promised grandfather we would return for the Christmas festivities perhaps we could be married then, make it a double celebration.'

To her astonishment he leapt to his feet yelling out in triumph. The sound of smashing crockery outside the door announced the unfortunate demise of the expected hot chocolate. Sebastian froze in mid-air and his look of horror sent Emily into a fit of giggles.

'For God's sake, Emily, desist. The poor girl will think you are laughing at her expense.'

Still laughing, she ran across to open the door. Outside a smiling parlour-maid was scooping up the mess. 'There is no hurry for my chocolate; I am sorry that Viscount Yardley startled you.'

'Not to worry, Miss Gibson. It's grand when a gentleman is so happy that he shouts it out like that.'

Emily closed the door and turned to face the man she had promised to spend the rest of her life with. He was watching the play of emotions cross her face.

'I have something here that belongs to you, my love.'

She held out her hand and he slipped the emerald ring back where it belonged.

We do hope that you have enjoyed reading this large print book.

Did you know that all of our titles are available for purchase?

We publish a wide range of high quality large print books including:
Romances, Mysteries, Classics
General Fiction
Non Fiction and Westerns

Special interest titles available in large print are:
The Little Oxford Dictionary
Music Book, Song Book
Hymn Book, Service Book

Also available from us courtesy of Oxford University Press:
Young Readers' Dictionary
(large print edition)
Young Readers' Thesaurus
(large print edition)

For further information or a free brochure, please contact us at:
Ulverscroft Large Print Books Ltd.,
The Green, Bradgate Road, Anstey,
Leicester, LE7 7FU, England.
Tel: (00 44) **0116 236 4325**
Fax: (00 44) **0116 234 0205**

RETURN TO
HEATHERCOTE MILL

Jean M. Long

Annis had vowed never to set foot in Heathercote Mill again. It held too many memories of her ex-fiancé, Andrew Freeman, who had died so tragically. But now her friend Sally was in trouble, and desperate for Annis' help with her wedding business. Reluctantly, Annis returned to Heathercote Mill and discovered many changes had occurred during her absence. She found herself confronted with an entirely new set of problems — not the least of them being Andrew's cousin, Ross Hadley . . .

THE COMFORT OF STRANGERS

Roberta Grieve

When Carrie Martin's family falls on hard times, she struggles to support her frail sister and inadequate father. While scavenging along the shoreline of the Thames for firewood, she stumbles over the unconscious body of a young man. As she nurses him back to health she falls in love with the stranger. But there is a mystery surrounding the identity of 'Mr Jones' and, as Carrie tries to find out who he really is, she finds herself in danger.

LOVE IN LUGANO

Anne Cullen

Suzannah Lloyd, sculptor and horti-culturist, arrives at an exhibition in Lugano which is showing some of her orchid sculptures. There she meets Mr Di Stefano, who offers her a job managing the grounds of his estate and orchid collection. Working closely with Mr Di Stefano's right hand man, Dante Candurro, she falls in love with him — but overhears his plans to steal the Di Stefano art collection. Feeling betrayed by further deception, can she ever learn to trust him?

THE CROSS AND THE FLAME

Roberta Grieve

While the Great Plague rages through London, Hester dreams of her sailor sweetheart Jonathan, despite being promised in marriage to her father's friend — the odious Thomas Latham. The deaths of her mother and baby brother bring guilty relief when the wedding is postponed. Then Jonathan returns to the news that Hester has died in the plague. Will he discover the deception before she is forced to marry a man who has no place in her heart?

MOTHER OF THE BRIDE

Zelma Falkiner

Kay Sheridan enjoys owning The Tea Cosy gift shop and tea-rooms. But for her, life has become quite hectic. A developer is threatening to disturb her tranquil village, and her landlord is demanding an increase in the rent of her premises that could close her down. Then her impetuous daughter surprises her with wedding plans, which will mean the return of her estranged husband. Will Kay be able to hide her unchanged love for him?

A LESSON IN LOVE

Shirley Heaton

Attractive widow Carol meets Paul on a campsite in France. After her return from holiday she discovers that he is the new tutor at her art class. Their friendship develops but, suspecting Paul may already have a partner, she is reluctant to make a commitment. During a visit to her health club, company director Simon introduces himself and later wines and dines her. Torn between the two, it takes a dangerous encounter for her to acknowledge her true love.